PROJECT FASHION
Prada Princesses

DON'T MISS THE OTHER BOOKS
IN THE SERIES:

Gucci Girls

Armani Angels

PROJECT FASHION
Prada Princesses

JASMINE OLIVER

SIMON PULSE
NEW YORK LONDON TORONTO SYDNEY

This book is a work of fiction. Any references to historical events, real people, or real locales are used fictitiously. Other names, characters, places, and incidents are the product of the author's imagination, and any resemblance to actual events or locales or persons, living or dead, is entirely coincidental.

SIMON PULSE

An imprint of Simon & Schuster Children's Publishing Division

1230 Avenue of the Americas, New York, NY 10020

Originally published in Great Britain in 2006 as *Cutting It: Prada Princesses* by Simon & Schuster UK Ltd, a CBS Company.

Published by arrangement with Simon & Schuster UK Ltd, a CBS Company.

The text of this book was set in Garamond 3.

Manufactured in the United States of America

First Simon Pulse edition August 2007

2 4 6 8 10 9 7 5 3 1

Library of Congress Control Number 2006940710

ISBN-13: 978-1-4169-3812-5

ISBN-10: 1-4169-3812-5

One

"Stop following me!" Marina said to Travis.

He zoomed in closer.

She stuck her tongue out at the camera lens. "I'm busy!"

Busy designing shoes for the end-of-year show. Looking wrecked without her lippy and mascara, tearing her blond hair out because she wouldn't be ready in time, and here was Sinead's boyfriend, Travis, filming every frazzled moment.

"I'm a fly-on-the-wall," he told her. "This is reality TV!"

"Give me a break!" Frankie groaned.

Travis had been following them 24/7 for the past two weeks, sticking his digi-cam in her face while she got made up for her fashion shoot, recording her as she swished down the catwalk in McCartney and Manolos.

"Look this way," Travis told her in the cramped dressing room while she squeezed into a bright blue Donna Karan number.

Frankie gave him the finger.

"Sweet!" he laughed, zooming in. "Do it again, Frankie! You look sexy when you're mad!"

"Switch that thing off!" Sinead sighed.

She had her feet up on Travis's sofa after a hard day at college. Two weeks to go before the First Year show and she was having a hard time convincing her tutors that she meant what she said.

"What do you mean—no fabrics?" Tristan Fox had frowned.

"No textiles, no leather, no jewelry—just body art," Sinead had insisted. She had this vision of her own body painted with amazing designs in henna and other natural dyes. Travis could photograph her close up, and those were the still images that would go into the show.

"This is a *fashion* college!" Tristan had reminded her.

"So? Body art is the way forward for fashion. Tattoos, piercings . . ." Sinead was sure she was right and Tristan had eventually given in.

"Why are you filming me?" she asked Travis now, hiding her face behind her hand. He'd been following her round the house, even into the bathroom until she slammed the door in his face.

"Because you're beautiful," he told her. *The lines on the palm of your hand, the pouty bottom lip, the soft blond halo of hair*. His camera adored the details.

"Stop, stop!" Sinead begged. She pulled a cushion over her face and Travis went on recording.

*

"*Why* is he?" Marina asked.

The girls had finally flopped on the sofa in the front room at Number 13 Walgrave Square. Frankie dangled her long, bare legs over one arm, her back against Sinead. "Yeah, why is he?" she echoed.

Sinead shook her head. "I've got no idea!"

"He says it's reality TV." Marina wiggled her toes in the soft pile of the cream rug. "He's so in-your-face about it. There I am, doing life-drawing, sewing straps, cutting leather. I look up, and Travis is invading my space with his pesky digi-cam!"

"Yeah, Sinead!" Frankie twiddled with a lock of her long dark hair. "You're his girlfriend. Can't you find out what he's up to?"

"I've asked him. He won't tell me. It must be something to do with his course." Sinead stared vacantly at the TV news. A car bomb had exploded somewhere. Some pop star had punched a cameraman in the face.

"Tell Travis I'll punch *him* in the face," Marina muttered.

Sinead and Frankie glanced sideways at their glossy, glitzy mate who would never risk chipping her nail gloss. They giggled.

"I'm knackered!" Sinead sighed.

"Me too."

"Me too."

"Only two weeks to go."

"Sinead, don't remind me!" Marina was still at an early stage with her shoe designs. Every day she was getting hassle from her tutors.

Frankie was way behind too. She'd had two well-paid fashion shoots in the past week, which meant that her college work had suffered. "Pressure, pressure!" she moaned.

"God, we've been here almost a year!" Sinead flicked the remote and the screen went dead. It seemed like only five minutes ago she was meeting Marina and Frankie for the first time, setting up home together in Sinead's mother's house, here in Walgrave Square.

Then she'd met Travis and fallen in love, and it was as if she'd known him all her life. "Time's weird," she murmured.

"Time's a slave driver!" Frankie complained. "Before I came to Central, I thought that fashion was about being creative and waiting for inspiration to strike. Now I can see it's all about meeting deadlines and ticking boxes and doing what your tutor tells you to do, or else."

Sinead shrugged. "What got into her?" she asked Marina.

"Dunno. What's she on?"

Frankie stood up and paced the floor. "Listen. I'm asking, what's so creative about doing stuff for this stupid end-of-year show? It's like they expect us to churn it out just so the college can show they've taught us properly."

Marina yawned. "That's life, babe."

"Who's churning stuff out?" Sinead wanted to know. "Not me, for starters." She'd burned the midnight oil designing the patterns she was going to paint over her whole body.

"Yeah, Frankie. You're only saying this because you've been

skiving off to do your Bed-Head jobs instead of putting in the work in the jewelry lab," Marina muttered.

Frankie frowned and stared at them. "You two are so . . ."

"So . . . what?" they demanded.

There was a long pause. The stress was getting to them all.

". . . Boring!" Frankie snapped. *Did I just say that? These are my best mates, for chrissakes!*

Marina's mouth fell open. "Did the little mouse just squeak?" She remembered the Frankie of eight months ago—so quiet she hardly ever spoke a word, so shy she couldn't go into the jewelry lab without having a panic attack.

"Boring!" Sinead gasped. She'd been accused of many things in her life—of being spoiled by her fashionista mother, of being moody and thin-skinned, vain and self-obsessed. But never boring!

But Frankie steamed on. "Yeah, you're both so predictable, trotting out the assignments on time like good little A-grade students. Didn't it ever strike you that you don't have to do it?"

"What—and get chucked out of college?" Marina said with a hollow laugh. "Yeah, my mum and dad would be really chuffed!"

"Hey, Travis," Frankie called out as she saw him come up the front path with his High Definition Sony. "We're having a cat-fight. Record this!"

He shuffled in, panning across the room from one girl to the other.

"Frankie's being a rebel," Sinead told the camera quietly, one eyebrow cocked.

"She's being a pain in the ass," Marina muttered.

Frankie told him to train the lens on her. "I'm being honest," she insisted. "I'm saying, why bother with silly qualifications and useless pieces of paper? All that matters is that you do the work that's important to you!"

"She's doing a James Dean, rebel-without-a-cause thing," Marina said in the background.

"She's pissed off," Sinead volunteered.

"Whatever!" Frankie hissed, eyes wide and unblinking as she made her announcement to camera. "Get this, Travis. On the record, I'm telling you that I'm boycotting the assessment!"

"Whoa!" Marina gasped.

"What are you saying?" Sinead demanded.

Frankie tossed her dark hair behind her shoulders. "I'm saying that Central Fashion College can stick their end-of-year show where the sun never shines!"

"Good job Tristan didn't hear what Frankie said earlier!" Marina leaned over and whispered to Sinead during their Head of Department's lecture.

Sinead glanced around. "Yeah, where is she?"

"Busy boycotting!" Marina mouthed, blushing as Tristan Fox glared at her.

"This assessment is vital," Tristan was saying, chest puffed out, doing his pompous senior lecturer bit. "As you know, this college year has provided you with a unique opportunity to generate and develop your own design ideas through practical and technical workshops. You've discovered your individual strengths."

"Blah-blah!" Sinead yawned. Maybe Frankie had a point.

Tristan strutted along the platform at the front of the lecture room. "Next year you will specialize in your chosen pathway, be it Fashion Design, Fashion Print, Knitwear, Marketing, Fashion History, and so on. But before then you will each be allocated a space in the end-of-year show to exhibit your special project."

"Yeah, yeah, we know!" Marina sighed. Tristan had an ego problem—it was enormous! He loved strutting his stuff in his crisp, pale pink shirt, with his slightly graying, well-cut hair, his Botoxed brow, and his mid-Atlantic accent.

"This is your chance to shine," he told his students, building to his climax. "Give us your energy, your glamour, your innovation! In return, we give you the space to showcase your work—it's up to you to make your mark!"

Rows of earnest faces nodded back at him.

At the back of the room, a figure stood in the doorway and clapped her hands in hollow applause.

"Frankie!" Marina and Sinead gasped.

Tristan Fox looked up and frowned. "Ah, Ms. McLerran!" he drawled. "How nice to see you!" He gave the signal that the lecture was over, then strode up the steps to collar her. "I've just been speaking to Claudia. She tells me she hasn't seen any proposals for your final project."

"That would be because I haven't done any," Frankie replied

flatly. She was wearing her anti-fashion statement of baggy black jumper and old jeans, no makeup, pale face, no jewelry.

Marina and Sinead whizzed up alongside and seized her by the arms. "Hey!" she protested.

"Sorry!" Sinead mumbled at the senior lecturer.

"Stress!" Marina explained.

Between them they half lifted gangly Frankie off the ground, turned her round, and herded her off down the corridor.

"Today is the deadline!" Tristan warned Frankie's back view. "See Claudia by the end of this afternoon!"

"She will!" Sinead promised, propelling Frankie away as fast as she could.

"Don't worry!" Marina gasped, smiling and nodding, then squeezing out a few words to Frankie between clenched teeth. "Shut it, Frankie! Don't say a word!"

"B-but! I want him to know I'm boycotting the show. Put me down, you two! You can't stop me!"

"Oh yes we can!" Sinead muttered, swinging through the double doors into the student café. "Just watch us!"

Marina sat Frankie down in the nearest seat. "Do you want to get thrown out?"

Frankie struggled and nodded.

"No, you don't!" Marina insisted, getting Frankie in a headlock. "Think about it. If you leave now, what will you do with the rest of your life?"

"Design jewelry," Frankie insisted. It was what she'd always wanted, dreamed of, longed for . . . but, at the end of the day, who needed the degree to go with the desire?

Sinead brought coffee and thrust it in front of Frankie. "Get real," she said sternly, seeing Travis-plus-camera out of the corner of her eye. "No way!" she warned him. "I mean it, Trav—this is serious!"

He zoomed in regardless.

"Listen!" Marina insisted, gradually releasing Frankie. "Most students would kill for a BA degree from Central. You can't just throw it away like a—like a used tissue!"

"Like I said—watch me!" Frankie muttered. "This place cramps my style. I go into the workshop and I feel I can't breathe!"

"Since when?" Sinead demanded. "Marina's right. A degree from Central gets you into the major fashion houses. Without it, you're just like hundreds of other wannabes."

Travis focused close up on Frankie's stubborn face. His lens captured the slight quiver of her bottom lip, the flicker of panic in her dark brown eyes.

"Leave me alone, why can't you?" she bleated.

Suddenly Marina switched tactics. She stood well back, arms folded. "Okay, then—walk!"

Sinead's wide gray eyes got wider.

Travis's lens picked up the spreading fear on Frankie's face.

"You leave with nothing!" Marina taunted. "And don't mind about Sinead and me—we'll find someone else to share the house with. Don't mind about your parents either—I expect they're used to having to worry about you!"

Frankie slumped forward, holding up her hand to hide from the camera.

"Nice one, babe!" Sinead whispered to Marina.

When Frankie looked up again, there was a deep frown line between her eyes. "Give me a break!" she pleaded with Travis.

"Are you staying, or are you going?" Marina was relentless.

Frankie wriggled on her chair, shying away from the lens.

"Staying or going?" Sinead demanded. "We need to know."

Deep breath. Don't cry. Bite the bullet and admit that you're shit-scared of failure. "Staying!" she muttered.

Sinead and Marina raised their fists in the air. "Result!" they shouted.

"But I haven't a clue what to put in the show!" Frankie wailed. "And I've got until the end of today to come up with something."

Sinead and Marina nodded.

"Help!" Frankie cried, staring at the camera. "Travis, you're my friend. Tell me, what in Christ's name am I going to do?"

Two

"So *your* girlfriend has Frankie in a headlock and *my* girlfriend is turning the emotional thumbscrews." In the technician's room behind the jewelry workshop, Travis gave Rob a blow-by-blow account of the latest crisis. "Honest, mate, it was like the Inquisition back there!"

"Marina and Sinead are two tough cookies!" Rob muttered, his goggles resting on the top of his head. "What's got into Frankie?"

Travis shrugged. "Hormones. Y'know what she's like."

"Yeah, women!"

"I recorded the whole thing on my HDR-HC1. I'll show you."

"Not now, mate. I told Claudia I'd have these opals polished up and ready for setting by midday."

Travis leaned back against the wall, arms folded. "I take it you're still online to help me edit this?"

"No sweat," Rob grunted, flicking the switch on the polisher.

"The idea is to cut the fights and the tears and the grungy bits into the glamour sequences—Frankie on the catwalk, Sinead and Marina partying. Kind of, Beauty and the Beast."

Rob grinned, pulling down his goggles over his eyes. "Did you tell the girls yet?"

"And ruin the whole thing? No way."

"Risky."

"How come?"

"They're gonna love you!" Rob knew how much Marina hated to be seen without her mascara and the rest of her war paint. He imagined Sinead and Frankie were the same.

"Nah, it'll be cool," Travis insisted.

"Hey, did I tell you I handed in my notice?" Rob said.

Travis swore. His jaw dropped.

Rob's expression was hidden by the goggles. "Yeah, mate. I'm sick of the job. I want to DJ full-time. Informed Claudia last week I was leaving."

"Christ!" Travis croaked. "It's like lemmings jumping over the bleeding cliff right now!"

"Today's my last day," Rob went on. "But don't mention it to Marina. I haven't told her yet."

"'Ne'er cast a clout 'til May is out!'" Frankie lay back on the grass under the blossom trees outside the students' union.

"What's that all about?" Sinead asked, sipping diet tonic water.

"My Yorkshire gran used to say it when I was a kid. Something about keeping your vest on, I think."

"Personally, I never wear a vest!" Marina said in her best posh voice.

"No, but this weather is so great." Sinead propped herself on one elbow and gazed up at the canopy of soft pink petals.

Marina spoiled the lazy, sunny mood with, "So, let's talk about Frankie's project."

"Aagh!" Frankie rolled onto her stomach and covered her ears.

Sinead tutted.

"What? She's got one hour and twenty minutes to decide what she's going to do." Marina had her sensible head on—the one she used to tell Rob he was drinking too much. "You heard what Tristan said this morning!"

Sinead leaned across and dragged Frankie's hands away from her ears.

"Hi!" Lee Wright called to the girls as he crossed the courtyard. He was on the second year Moving Images course with Travis.

Sinead and Marina waved back, while Frankie clamped her hands to her ears again.

Lee shrugged and disappeared into the building.

"Pity about Lee. He's so-ooh . . ." Sinead sought for the right word.

". . . Geeky!" Frankie broke in, letting them know she could hear every word.

". . . *Nice!*" Sinead and Marina sighed.

Frankie had been out with Lee twice—once to see a Brad Pitt

movie, once to the pub. ("We were never an item!" Frankie would insist afterward.)

"Nice—schmice!" she muttered now, sitting up and tugging at her V-neck sweater to expose her skinny shoulders to the spring sunshine. "Oh, won't someone please give me an idea for my project?"

"Hey, Ms. Inspiration, what was all that stuff about creativity you were spouting earlier?" Marina reminded her.

Frankie groaned. "I don't have a single thought in my head. I'm going to fail this course!" she declared. This year she'd made jewelry out of chiffon and seed pearls, plastic buttons and wooden beads, silver and semiprecious stones. She'd gone ethnic, funky, nautical, and Native American—you name it, she'd been there. But right now, at the precise minute she had to come up with a new theme, her mind was a blank.

"Hmmm," Sinead said quietly. No one heard her.

"What about your designs based on graffiti art?" Marina reminded her. "Didn't Claudia say they were cool?"

"Yeah, but I need something completely new for the show."

"Hmmm."

Marina threw Sinead a sideways glance. "What are you 'hmm-ming' at?" Then, "Hey, is that the time? I've got life-drawing. I gotta go!" She was up and gone in a flash, leaving Sinead and Frankie under the blossom trees.

"Hmmm. Listen," Sinead began. "You know my body-art thing?"

"Yeah, I like it. It's pushing the envelope." Frankie always expected Sinead to come up with a unique approach—no textiles and designing onto naked flesh was definitely a Sinead Harcourt special.

Sinead thought for a while, sitting with her knees hunched to her chest, her hands clasped around her knees. "How do you fancy making it a *joint* project?"

Frankie was immediately drawn in. "In what way?"

"*I* design the natural dye motifs. *You* design the jewelry to go with them. Bracelets, ankle chains, maybe the odd body piercing. After all, I'm prepared to suffer for my art."

Frankie nodded. "Got you."

"I'm basing my stuff on traditional patterns and abstract shapes, so the jewelry should echo that."

"Silver? Or maybe silver and enamel. I'd be into that. But would they let us?"

"What—do a joint project?" Sinead tilted her head from side to side. "Yeah, why not? Tristan said we had to be innovative!"

It was Frankie's turn to think it through. "We'd still get Travis to take the photographs of you, with all the right angles and lighting and close-ups and stuff. We'd each do a portfolio of designs and theory. They could grade us separately . . ."

". . . Or together!" Sinead suggested.

"Cool!" Frankie felt a weight lifting from her shoulders. It was as if she could suddenly sit up straight and breathe. "Hey, Sinead, this could really work!"

"*Will* work!" Sinead promised, her eyes sparkling.

"Turquoise enamel on silver!" Frankie enthused. "The color is good against your skin tone. And I could design a piece that combines a necklace with an arm band around the top of your arm, coming diagonally across your shoulder like this . . ."

". . . With colored patterns on my cheek and neck, intertwining with the jewelry."

"Yeah, cool!" Frankie could see it in her imagination—the perfect design!

"So?" Sinead asked after a short pause.

Frankie sprang up and flicked her hair back. "So I'm going to see Claudia!" she said, dashing across the grass. "Wait here. She's so–oh going to love this idea!"

"Why the grim face?" Jack Irvine asked Marina in the life-drawing class. He'd been watching her work with pastels, blocking in the light and shadow on the torso of the male model who was posing in a standing position, his back toward her.

Marina shaded in the space between the model's spine and shoulder blade. Then she captured the line and angle of his strong shoulders. "Guess what," she muttered. "They gave me a minuscule space to display my shoe designs, and it's tucked away in a corner."

"So, Ms. Kent is not happy!" The life-drawing tutor pointed to an unworked area on her A1 paper. "You need to address that," he remarked.

"I am so not happy!" she sighed. "I work my balls off all year long, trying to impress Tristan with strappy sandals, espadrilles, wedgies, flip-flops, court shoes in leather, suede, satin. I go ethnic, then I go eighties glam. I work forever on these end-of-year, Hollywood-influenced designs. And what do I get? A display area the size of a . . . shoebox—ha-ha!"

Jack laughed. "I told you, your talent was wasted in fashion design. You're a Fine Art student who lost her way!"

"Thanks!" she muttered.

As the tutor ordered the model to take a break, Marina stepped back from her work.

Even she had to admit that the drawing wasn't bad. The naked torso covered the entire A1 sheet. She'd captured it with vigorous strokes that showed its strength and suppleness.

"I mean it," Jack Irvine insisted. "Don't tell Tristan Fox I said so, but I think you should seriously consider switching courses at the start of next year."

The comment hit home. It raised little flutters of excitement in her chest. *What if . . . ?* she thought. *What if I really do have a talent for drawing and painting, and I'm not just some little airhead who worships at the altar of high fashion? I could switch to Fine Art and be a proper artist!*

"We need people like you, Marina," Jack said, hands in the pockets of his baggy, paint-stained trousers. He stared hard at her work, considering the quality of her mark-making and composition.

I could be an artist and starve in an attic! she went on to herself.

I could be covered in paint, like Jack, and stink of linseed oil! People would say I was talented but no one would buy my work. Critics would rubbish me. Frankie would be strutting her stuff on the catwalks of New York *and Paris. Sinead would shun me 'cause I looked like a tramp! I'd be Marina-no-mates!*

Jack Irvine seemed to read her mind. "Ah yes, I forgot," he said, turning his back and walking away. "A life of poverty and obscurity doesn't appeal to a glitzy glamour girl like you."

"Hang on, I never said that!" she protested.

Then she sighed and shook her head. *Get real!* she told herself. *Take your shoebox space and make the most of it. That's why you're here at Central. Fashion is your bible. There's no getting away from that.*

Three

"Do you want me to fail my course?" Travis asked Sinead.

There was tension between them that could be cut with a knife. So what was new?

Sinead was hiding in the loo at his place. "If you don't turn that camera off, I'm leaving!"

He kept the digi-cam running, waiting for her to come out.

"I mean it, Travis!" She couldn't move without being recorded. Next thing, he'd be in the loo with her, filming as she peed. And Sinead was a private person. "Is it turned off?" she demanded.

Travis caught a shot of her head as she peered around the door. "What's the big deal?" he asked.

Sinead came out, eyes blazing. "The big deal, as you put it, is that I feel as if I'm being spied on 24/7! I'm not comfortable, Travis. I mean it!"

"It's art," he explained. "I'm shooting reality TV."

"Go shoot it somewhere else," she snapped. "Next thing, you'll be filming us in bed together, making porn and calling it art!"

The camera wobbled as Sinead pushed past Travis on the landing and ran angrily downstairs. At last he gave in and switched it off. "Hey, are you really mad?" he asked.

"Yeah, really!" Downstairs in the kitchen she found a mirror image of Marina and Rob arguing.

". . . What do you mean, you quit your job?" Marina's voice went up a couple of octaves.

Rob grabbed a beer from the fridge. "I handed in my notice. I'm not going back to the jewelry lab."

"So what are you going to live on—fresh air?" God, how come she sounded like her mother all of a sudden?

"I plan to DJ full-time. And I'm working on promoting new bands."

Marina swallowed hard. "You don't think that's kind of risky?"

Travis had followed Sinead downstairs. "Hand me a beer, mate," he said to Rob.

Sinead lined up alongside Marina. "Men!" she muttered.

"I'm sick of being a wage slave," Rob said.

"But you're only twenty-three! You've a whole life ahead of you to consider. Anyway, how come you never said anything to me?" Marina wanted to know. "Maybe we could've discussed it first."

"Yeah!" Sinead said to Travis. "For example, when people make reality TV, they usually explain it to their victims *before* they turn on the camera!"

"Whoa!" Rob and Travis said, backing up against the fridge.

The girls advanced together. "Isn't that what relationships are about?" Marina demanded. "Y'know—couples talk, they agree on things, then they do them."

"In that order!" Sinead insisted.

Marina stared at Rob in his leather jacket, his biker helmet thrown to one side on the kitchen worktop. Her problem was, every time she looked at his gorgeous face with his short dark hair and always that faint stubble on his chin, she melted.

Sinead blinked then turned away from Travis. "You should've asked," she muttered.

"You would've said no," he pointed out logically. Travis loved Sinead, but she was high maintenance. "And the whole point is to get you three girls on camera in a spontaneous way. Explaining the whole thing would totally ruin it."

"I feel used," Sinead complained. She walked out of the kitchen, down the hallway, to the front door.

"Hey," Marina told Rob. "I suppose you might be right."

"You do?"

She went up and put her arms around him. "You're a cool DJ."

"And I got Bad Mouth a big gig in the City Hall for October," he told her. "The guys put me on a percentage."

Marina smiled then kissed him. "I love you, Rob Evans," she said.

"Don't walk off," Travis warned Sinead.

She stopped at the door. "I have to go home and work."

"I thought we were going out for something to eat."

"I'm not hungry."

"Sinead, don't go!"

"I have to work."

Travis took her by the hand. "Sorry," he said.

She nodded briefly. She studied his face like a map—the straight contours of his eyebrows, the deep pools of his eyes. "I'll see you tomorrow," she said.

Everywhere people were quitting.

As Marina put on her makeup, getting ready for work behind the bar at Escape, she replayed in her mind Frankie wanting to give up her course and now Rob resigning from his technicianship. Was that a word? Anyhow, he'd left, and guess what—she was now going out with a professional DJ!

On went the eyeliner and mascara, followed by the fake tan. So far this year there hadn't been a chance to soak up the sun and get the real thing. Never cast a what-was-it? A clout, or a vest or something.

I could quit fashion and take up serious art, Marina told her reflection. She'd already given up blogging the previous month, signing off with a Bugs Bunny cartoon flourish—**"That's all folks!"**—after Sinead had told her only airheads blogged.

"Who wants the whole world to know your business?" Sinead had asked.

Talking of Sinead and giving up bad habits, Marina realized that her super-skinny friend hadn't eaten for days and now wouldn't touch a calorie in case it killed her.

Okay, so Frankie almost chucked in her course, Rob has quit his job, and now Sinead has given up food—that's all we need! she thought, brushing on her lip gloss. *Anorexia, here we come!*

Ready to go, she tip-tapped downstairs in her high heels and poked her nose into the front room, where Sinead sat surrounded by sheets of A4. "Do you fancy calling in to Escape later on?" she asked, thinking that maybe she could ram a small slice of pizza down her thin friend's throat.

"Might do," Sinead said, without looking up.

Marina knew not to force the issue. "Okay, see you."

She bumped into Frankie on the front path. "Rob quit his job," she told her hurriedly. "Sinead is wasting away. I'm late. Catch you on the flip!"

Sinead looked up from her designs as Frankie clattered into the room and flung down her bag. After the row with Travis she felt spaced out and detached from everything that was going on.

"How's it hangin'?" Frankie asked, flopping onto the sofa.

"Daniella just called," Sinead replied. "Apparently she can get me a summer placement with Emanuel Ungaro in Milan."

"Oh wow! How come?" Frankie would kill for a chance like that. She rested her head against a cushion.

Sinead shrugged. "You know my mother. She has connections."

"Yeah, with every fashion house in Europe!" Frankie sighed. She loved Ungaro's style—the Italian excess and eye for shimmery detail.

"Or Prada," Sinead added. "Daniella says it's up to me."

Frankie made a gagging gesture. "It makes me sick. The world of fashion is Sinead Harcourt's oyster and she's not even happy about it!"

"Yeah, sorry." Sinead managed a half-grin. "I should act more grateful, shouldn't I?"

"Ye-ah!" Frankie sat up. "Listen, I'm trying to get a work experience place with Sophia Kokosalaki. I don't suppose Daniella could . . ."

Sinead nodded. "I'll ask her."

"Thanks."

"No worries." Sinead was surprised by Frankie's choice. She always had her down as Marni or John Galliano—more quirky and mussed-up than angel who fell to earth. "Hey, how did your meeting with Claudia go?"

Frankie gave a thumbs-up. "Cool. We can do it."

"We can?" Sinead grinned. "Will we be assessed together or separately?"

"Together."

"Cool! What did Claudia say exactly?"

"She said no one had done this kind of thing before. But she needs to see designs by the beginning of next week and a detailed critique of why we want to do it." Sitting cross-legged on the floor beside Sinead, Frankie began to sift through the experimental drawings scattered across the rug. "I like this one," she remarked, choosing a motif that wound across the shoulder and down the arm like an intricate strap. "I could design my arm band to start abovc the elbow and meet your patterns along the collarbone. Is Travis standing by to take the pictures?"

The name brought a frown to Sinead's face. "We're not speaking," she confessed.

"Since when?"

"Since about two hours ago."

Frankie was used to Sinead and Travis's on-off relationship. And Travis was a good mate of Frankie's. "No problem. I'll fix it up," she promised. "If we work fast, I should have something designed and made by this time next week. Then we could do the photo shoot."

Sinead nodded. "We should work together this weekend. How about Saturday?"

"Sorry, no can do." Frankie shook her head. "I've got a modeling job."

"Where?"

"Don't know." Frankie checked the text message she'd had from the Bed-Head agency. She read it once, then twice. "Paris!" she gasped. "Hey, I didn't read that part before!"

"Frankie's going to Paris," Sinead told Marina in a lull between customers at Escape.

She'd come into town to avoid Travis, who'd been texting her all evening, asking to talk. Speak 2moro, she'd replied, before slipping out of the back door. She'd deliberately avoided his house overlooking the square.

"You look terrible," Marina had told her when she'd sat on a bar stool and ordered a sparkling water. Sinead could change from bright-eyed innocence to washed-out wreck in a nanosecond. And not eating definitely wasn't helping. "I'm worried about you," she'd added.

Sinead had shook her head. "I'm fine."

"Paris?" Marina asked, noticing that Travis and Rob had come into the bar.

"For twenty-four hours, on a modeling job. Another girl on Bed-Head's books had to cancel, so Frankie lucked out again."

"Paris!" Marina echoed. Paris in spring—sunlit street cafés, sailing up the Seine, moonlight, and music . . . "Rob, when you're rich and famous, will you take me to Paris?" she called.

Sinead swung round on her stool, saw Travis, and realized it was too late to slip away. "Hey," she said quietly, feeling her stomach flip.

"Hey," he replied.

Marina pulled Rob off to one side so Travis and Sinead could talk. "I'm worried about her," she repeated. "Frankie says she hasn't eaten. Look how thin she is."

Rob glanced along the bar. "She's always skinny."

"She's stressed out," Marina insisted, handing him a beer. "And Travis filming her every second doesn't help."

"He says he's stopped." Glancing at his watch, Rob told her he had to go. He swigged from the bottle, leaned across the bar, and kissed her. "Got to see a man about a dog."

"Meaning?"

He grinned. "Tell you later—if it works out."

"Thanks!" Kissing him back, Marina went off to serve another customer.

"See, no camera!" Travis told Sinead. He sat on a stool beside her.

She nodded. There was still that weird barrier between her and the world—like toughened glass, invisible but unbreakable.

"Are you okay?"

Another nod. Then a feeling suddenly welling up, as if she was about to cry. But that was stupid. She fought back the tears.

"Talk to me," he whispered, reaching out to take her hand. Travis's stomach was twisted into knots at the sight of Sinead perched on the stool like a baby bird, all eyes and helplessness. She never grew less beautiful in his eyes—only deeper and more complicated. And yes, he should have asked her about the reality filming, and he should have respected her privacy.

Sinead took a sip of water. "I'm tired."

"Come home with me."

She let him help her down off the stool. She stood for a second, head swimming.

Along the bar, Marina saw Sinead sway backward. "Travis!" she warned.

Sinead saw the glinting bottles on the shelf behind the bar turn into weird amber and ruby prisms. She grasped at the edge of the granite bar top. Then her knees gave way and she slid to the floor.

After a few sips of water and the attentions of a nearby medical student, Sinead was soon sitting up.

"When did you last eat?" the medical student asked her.

Sinead gazed round the tiny staff room beside the Ladies. She made out the face of the stranger talking to her, and behind him, Travis and Marina. "Sorry!" she breathed.

"How long ago?" the medic insisted.

"Breakfast." She'd had a boiled egg, but nothing since.

The student shook his head. "Fainting is the body's way of telling her she's not taking on enough fuel," he told Travis. "Is she your girlfriend?"

Travis nodded. He was struck down by guilt.

"Get her to eat," the medic advised before he left. "If she won't, make sure she sees her GP."

"I'm fine!" Sinead insisted, making a big effort to stand up. "There is absolutely nothing wrong with me!"

"Phone call for you, Marina!" Marina's manager stuck his head around the door and dragged her away.

"Look after her," Marina told Travis. She went to take the call.

"Marina, it's me."

She stuck a finger in one ear to drown out the bar noise. "Hi, Mum."

"Sorry to bother you at work."

Marina's mother called once a week, on a Sunday afternoon, for the how-are-you, do-you-need-any-money chat. She never phoned her at work. "What's wrong?" Marina asked.

"Nothing. Don't worry. I just thought I'd better let you know."

There was a weird evasiveness in her mum's voice. Whoa, this must be serious—an illness, an accident, or her dad leaving. Something Marina didn't want to hear. "I'm busy, Mum!"

"Yes, sorry, love. But you need to know this—I've been trying to contact your dad. I can't get him to answer his phone."

"What d'you mean? Where is he?"

"He's in West Africa, doing advisory work for a water company out there. He flew out on Monday."

Oh, just work. Not so bad then. Her dad often flew all over the world on business trips. "What happened? Did his phone go dead?"

"Well, he's not answering it, so I rang his boss. They tried to contact him, but it was no-go for them too."

"Oh." Marina's mind clicked and went blank. She didn't know what to say.

"Are you there?" her mum asked. "Listen, love, I don't think there's any need to worry. I just thought you should know."

Marina fought to listen over the sound track that was blaring through the speakers. Her dad was in Africa. He was out of contact. "You mean he's vanished?"

"No, no!" her mum soothed. "Nothing like that. His boss has contacted the British Embassy out there. They're going to track him down and tell him to get in touch. It's probably some technical hitch, a loss of signal, a breakdown in communications that they can easily sort out. I'll let you know as soon as they hear from him."

My dad has vanished. He's missing, probably in some war zone, with bombs exploding and people getting shot. That's what her mother was really telling her. "Okay, Mum, thanks," Marina said.

"Like I said, don't worry."

"Do you want me to come home?" she asked as an afterthought.

"No! Definitely not. Stay where you are. You hear?"

"Okay."

"I've got to go now, Marina. I'll ring you as soon as I hear anything."

"Okay, bye."

The phone went dead. The music blasted through her head.

Four

"Where's Rob?" On Friday morning, before she left for Paris, Frankie charged into the technician's room at college and bumped into Lee Wright. "Oh yeah, I forgot—Rob left!"

Lee didn't step back quickly enough from the high-speed crash. Instead, he grinned as Frankie's bag tipped upside down and the contents skidded across the floor. Together they rescued her hair-brush, mobile phone, passport, and stash of loose change.

"Thanks!" Frankie mumbled, on her hands and knees. "I needed a tiny pair of pliers. Rob keeps them in a drawer some-where."

Lee dropped the last coins back into her bag then reached for the tool. "Are these them?"

"Thanks. What are you grinning at?" she demanded.

"Nothing. You. See you, Frankie!" Lee sauntered off and was soon at the far side of the workshop, talking to Suzy Atkins, a fashion student from the second year.

What's funny? Frankie wondered. She used the pliers to tighten a link in the fastening for the prototype arm band she'd been designing for the project with Sinead.

"It's only a rough idea," she explained, taking the arm band to show Sinead on the top-floor library. "Can I leave it with you?"

"Sure." Sinead had gotten into college early and had been researching some more designs for her body art. She looked up at Frankie. "Hey, shouldn't you be in Paris?"

"Give me a chance! I fly out to Charles de Gaulle airport at three this afternoon." Frankie liked the way that sounded—*I fly out . . . Charles de Gaulle . . . !* She rolled it round her tongue.

"Get out of here!" Sinead sighed. "And take some photos while you're there. I love Paris!"

"Sure. Eiffel Tower. Notre Dame. Hunky guys in blue-and-white-striped T-shirts and berets. Will that do?"

"Tack-tastic!" Sinead joked. "Hey, have a cool time!"

"Will do!" Frankie promised, dashing off.

An hour later, she had collected the details of her assignment from the snooty receptionist at the Bed-Head Agency, snatched a take-out cappuccino from Costa Coffee, and was on her way to check in at the airport.

To be honest, she thought, sitting in the departure lounge, *I'm glad to get away for twenty-four hours.*

A guy in the seat opposite, with a deep tan, big muscles, and long, sun-bleached hair, was unashamedly copping an eyeful of

Frankie's low-slung hipster shorts, short white shirt, and big wedgie espadrilles.

She ignored him. *Pressure, pressure!* she thought. Back at Walgrave Square, there was Sinead worrying about her end-of-year designs, her relationship with Travis, her weight—you name it, Sinead worried about it.

"Passengers for the BA flight to Paris, Charles de Gaulle, please go to departure gate 21, where boarding is about to begin!"

Frankie grabbed her belongings. *And now poor Marina!* she thought. It was harder to spot when Marina had a problem—she didn't let it show in her face and body language the same way that Sinead did—but she'd mentioned to Frankie that her dad was out of contact with her mum, then shrugged, and said she was sure it was a temporary blip, that was all.

"I can tell you one thing—Mum definitely didn't want me at home with her," Marina had confided, perching on the edge of Frankie's bed the night before.

"I expect she knows you've got your end-of-year deadlines to meet," Frankie had said.

But Marina had shaken her head. "No. It wasn't that. My mother's idea of dealing with a problem is to keep us kids out of it. She thinks me and my brother can't handle it, like we're still five years old."

Then they'd talked about mothers in general.

"Sinead's mum acts like Sinead is her sister—she involves her in everything that's going on in her life," Marina had pointed out.

"Yeah, I wouldn't like that." Frankie recognized that Daniella Harcourt was fabulously fashionable and cool, but she didn't act the way you wanted your mother to act. With Daniella, there was always a trauma or a crisis.

Marina had nodded. "The problem with mine is the opposite—you have to squeeze information out of her. It's like getting blood out of a stone."

"Mine's somewhere in between," Frankie had decided, realizing now that she hadn't even had time to phone her mum and tell her about this latest modeling job.

`Am flying to Paris`, she texted, then switched off her phone and boarded the plane.

The man with the tan parked his backpack in the overhead locker and squeezed his muscles into the seat beside her.

No news. Marina checked her messages before she went into the painting studio. There was no official class this afternoon, but she wanted to carry on working on the pastel sketch she'd begun earlier in the week.

No news is good news. Except when your dad's phone is down in an unstable country swarming with rebels and fanatics, not to mention biblical plagues of locusts.

"Do you know the work of Lucian Freud?" Jack Irvine asked, appearing out of nowhere.

Marina guessed he spent his entire life dressed in baggy, paint-spattered trousers and an old T-shirt. His gray beard had tinges of yellow ochre and cobalt blue. "Nope," she replied, taking up a stick of burnt umber and getting ready to block in part of the background to her sketch.

"He's an artist you should look at," Jack insisted. "There's an attention to detail and a strength of line that I'm sure you'd like."

"Lucian Freud. Any relation to Sigmund?" Marina asked, by way of conversation. Jack was hard work. Why couldn't he tell a joke or just talk about the weather once in a while?

"Yes, actually."

"Oh!" *Piss off!* she thought. *Stop peering over my shoulder like the bad-tempered dwarf in Snow White. Heigh-ho, heigh-ho, and off to work we go!*

Jack studied her latest drawing. "I really think you should transfer to Fine Art," he said quietly. "But you would need to get together a decent portfolio first."

Marina stared at him. "I'll think about it!" she said.

"Are we talking or not talking?" Travis asked Sinead.

He'd gone round to her place after college to check on how she was after her fainting fit the night before.

"Have you brought your Sony?"

"No."

"Then we're talking." She'd stayed in bed late, until Marina and Frankie had left for college. When she'd got up the first thing she'd done was to go and weigh herself. Cool—she'd lost another whole pound.

Travis moved her sheets of design work and cozied up to her on the sofa. "So, are we going into town later?"

Sinead drew a deep breath. "I don't know, Travis. I'm not really into that right now. I'm too busy."

Then she realized it was Friday and she ought to get into chill mode for his sake. "Okay. Where do you want to go?"

"We could eat at the Thai place then maybe meet up with Rob and Marina." As Travis said the "eat" word, he realized it would send Sinead off on an avalanche of reasons why not. *No time. I don't like Thai food. I've already eaten, thanks*. None of which would be true.

But, "I'm not hungry," was all she said.

Quickly he changed the subject. "So when do you and Frankie want to begin shooting for your show?"

She kissed his cheek for letting her off the food hook. "Maybe Wednesday or Thursday of next week." By then she aimed to lose another pound or two, so the camera couldn't pick up any unsightly bulges. The outline of her body would look totally toned.

"I'll sort out some rolls of film and set up the studio lights," he promised, moving in for a serious kiss.

Close to, Sinead's pale gray eyes blurred, her mouth softened, and her skin felt like velvet. God, he couldn't help himself, he really did love her.

Off the plane, onto the tarmac, and into the psychedelic sixties web of moving walkways at Charles de Gaulle, Frankie would have to rush to reach her hotel before dark. She hopped onto a train that would take her to the center of Paris, only to find that the blond guy with the six-pack and the bulging backpack was still close on her heels.

He stood next to her in the swaying carriage. "Are you following me?" she accused.

"Only if you want me to." The voice was deep and Aussie, or maybe Kiwi. There was a warm smile to go with it.

"What are you doing in Paris?" Frankie asked, basking in the smile.

"Traveling through. I'm on my way to Rome to meet up with my brother. How about you?"

They rattled through the outskirts of the city—gray and tatty, covered in graffiti like any other. "Work," she replied. Her hotel was in Montmartre. The fashion shoot began on the steps of Sacré Coeur at six-thirty next morning.

"Hey, you don't look old enough. I had you down as a freewheeling student, not part of the great global workforce."

"I work part time," she explained as the train screeched to a halt in Gare du Nord.

"What d'you do?" the hunky backpacker asked.

Frankie picked up her bag from the floor and slung it over her shoulder. The train door slid open. "You won't believe it!" she grinned, thinking that maybe an espresso coffee with him out of one of those tiny, chunky dark green cups with the gold rim before she settled down in her hotel might not be an altogether bad idea.

*

Rob knocked on the door of the life-drawing studio. "Can I come in?" he mouthed at Marina through the small pane of glass.

She nodded. "Sorry—there's no naked model for you to gawk at," she told him.

"Shame." He came up behind her and admired the drawing she was working on. "Wow, that's—cool!"

She stood back from the drawing board. "You say the nicest things, Rob Evans."

"No, I mean it. You should get it framed and sell it. Then you can keep me in the style . . ."

". . . To which you're accustomed!" she grinned. "Look at you! You're so *not* accustomed to living in any kind of style!" Putting down her pastels, Marina threatened to smudge Rob's face with her messy, multicolored fingers.

Rob glanced down at his beaten-up leather jacket. "What d'you mean? I do effortless boho chic pretty well!"

"More biker heavy metal."

"James Dean *Rebel Without a Cause*."

"Marlon Brando *On the Waterfront*." They listed their favorite movies from the fifties.

"Let's go!" Rob took Marina's hand and led her out of the studio. He glanced over his shoulder at his mussed-up, color-streaked, dressed-down girl.

"You're different from when we first met," he told her.

"In a good or a bad way?" She thought she knew the answer, but it would be cool to hear it anyway.

"Come here," he mumbled, turning and giving her a giant hug. "The best way. Did I tell you I went to see a guy in local radio?"

"A man about a dog?" she recalled, soaking in the feel and smell of his Rob-jacket.

"About a late-night slot fronting a show that introduces new bands. This guy is the producer."

Marina stepped back and studied his face to check if he was serious. "And?"

"I'm on the short list," he told her. "Come on, honey, let's celebrate!"

Am in Paris with hunky Kiwi, Frankie texted first Marina and then Sinead.

"Frankie's in Paris with a Kiwi!" Sinead told Marina when they met up in Escape. It was ten thirty. She and Travis had found Marina and Rob celebrating in the bar where Marina worked.

"I know. She texted me."

Sinead sat down at the bar. "I called her. His name's Ian. He plays rugby. Did your mum hear from your dad yet?"

Marina shook her head. She didn't want to talk about it, but in her head she'd already imagined the worst. She'd relived all the news footage of hostages in blindfolds with their hands tied behind their backs, of flood and famine, of earthquake and disease, and boy, was she scared.

"Ring her," Sinead urged.

"I can't. I have to wait until she calls me."

Sinead nodded. "Hey, it'll be fine. Parents do this to you—they screw you up and make you worry about them. Then they call and suddenly everything's hunky-dory!" After all, Daniella did it to her every other day.

"You're right," Marina agreed. Her dad could look after himself. Whenever he went on these trips to Africa he took a local guide with him who spoke the language, and he had the backup of a huge multinational water company behind him. So she changed the subject. "Listen, Rob's got a chance of landing the old Jon Savage slot. He's talked to the producer. They really like him. He has to go in on Monday for a formal interview."

"Fantastic! He'd better not forget his mates when he's a world-famous DJ!"

Early next morning Frankie skipped the croissants and headed up the hill toward the domed white church. The cobbled streets and squares were empty except for a trundling machine that swooshed water onto the roads and scrubbed them clean.

Her phone took a message. One new text. Options. View.

Thanx 4 last nite. Ian xx

She texted back. And u xx

Ian was a nice guy—not complicated, what you saw was what

you got. And she'd been tempted by the drop-dead gorgeous bod.

Over coffee and then a couple of glasses of wine in a dark bar on the Left Bank, he'd told her all about himself—how he'd played rugby for New Zealand juniors, then got a leg injury that had ruled out a professional career in the game. He was twenty-three and traveling. He'd been to the Far East and was now doing Europe.

She'd told him that she'd fallen into modeling by accident. Her real passion was for making jewelry, but she was under pressure from her tutors to deliver the goods for an end-of-year show, and she wasn't sure she'd make the grade.

"I'm booked into a little B & B by the Moulin Rouge," she'd told him when he'd asked where she was staying. Should she invite him back?

"I'll walk you there," he'd offered.

The streets of Paris on a spring night, holding the hand of a handsome guy, trying out her schoolgirl French as they'd asked the way to Montmartre.

The River Seine and the twinkling lights of the bateaux mouches sailing slowly under the romantic bridges. The flying buttresses of Notre Dame.

"Are you for real?" he'd asked her, his arm around her shoulder, staring down at the dark water from a bridge. "Or am I dreaming?"

Frankie had laughed. "I'm a girl you met in an airport," she reminded him. And she'd decided not to invite him in because if she had, she would have regretted it next morning, and because she'd had enough of guys who were in transit, like Wim, who'd two-timed her and laughed at her for being naïve. She and Ian had kissed on the doorstep of her pokey hotel. A nice kiss to remember each other by.

And now the texts. `Cool. Have a nice life, Ian.`

"Are you Frankie McLerran?" A harassed woman in a waterproof jacket approached her at the base of the broad steps to Sacré Coeur. "I'm Nina, the stylist. We need you in the makeup van pronto."

Frankie stared in the mirror.

They'd applied a mask of makeup—dark eyes, heavy eyebrows, pale lips. Her long dark hair was pinned up under an exotic Philip Treacy hat of trailing white ostrich feathers. And they'd zipped her into an Armani off-the-shoulder sequinned jacket, ruched and covered in crystals, with a long, pearl gray satin skirt, then slipped her feet into a pair of high-heeled D & G diamante sandals. Show Girl at 7:00 a.m.

"Ready to rumble?" Nina inquired, tired, frayed at the edges, and full of old clichés. She opened the caravan door.

The morning light was still pale, the marble steps up to the church shimmery and deserted. Frankie struck a pose. The photographer twirled the dials on his camera.

I'm in Paris! Frankie told herself. *I'm in the pages of magazines like* Harpers and Queen. *Life doesn't get much better than this!*

Five

"This isn't good enough!" Claudia Brown told Frankie. She pushed her designs back across the desk. "How long did these take you?"

Frankie shrugged.

"A couple of hours max," the tiny tutor guessed. She made up for her five-feet two inches with the voice of a sergeant major and eyes that pierced right through you. "In fact, you probably threw them together on the bus on your way into college."

"I'm still at an early stage. I have to develop them," Frankie objected weakly. The weekend had taken it out of her and left her feeling wrecked.

"Early stage, my ass!" Standing up from her desk, Claudia stalked out into the corridor to the coffee machine. She came back into her office with two steaming plastic cups. "You look as if you need this," she muttered.

Frankie took a sip. "I'll work on them all day today," she promised.

"You can work on them until the end of next year—they still

won't come right." The jewelry tutor never minced her words. "Frankie, these designs lack imagination. They have no flair. They're never going to be any good."

There was a long, heavy silence. In spite of the strong coffee, Frankie's energy seemed to have slumped then seeped out through the soles of her feet.

"Where were you this weekend?"

"Paris."

"Doing what?"

"Modeling for a spread in *Harpers*."

More silence. Then, "Congratulations, Frankie." Claudia's voice was flat, her sharp features expressionless.

"For what?" Frankie didn't want to hear the answer. She gathered the sheets of paper and stuffed them into her denim bag.

"For abandoning a promising career as a jewelry designer before the end of your first year."

Ouch! Frankie stood up, ready to leave.

Claudia's gimlet eyes followed her every move. "Is that it?" she inquired.

Hot tears came to Frankie's eyes. She felt she'd let Claudia down big time. On top of which, she would have to confess to Sinead that their joint project had bitten the dust. "I'm sorry."

"Sorry? Aren't you even going to fight back?"

"No. You're right. These designs are crap."

Claudia let her reach the door before she spoke again. "I understand what's going on here, believe me."

Frankie paused. She'd managed to control the tears. Okay, so Claudia was right and her dream was dead, but right now she couldn't cope with sympathy.

"Sit!" the tutor ordered.

Robotically Frankie returned to her seat.

"I know why you've been drawn in. There's the glamour of modeling for a start," Claudia went on. "Then there's the flattering illusion that physical beauty really does turn you into someone special."

It took Frankie a while to figure out what she meant. She shook her head.

"Yes," Claudia insisted. "I'm not saying you're vain, my dear. Not more so than one would expect in a beautiful girl of your age. But you do have the looks of a supermodel, and, let's face it, that must be hard to deal with."

"I don't think about it," Frankie protested. "They dress me up and point the camera at me. It's only a job."

Claudia studied her for a long while. "It's an incredible line to take, but I believe you're sincere," she acknowledged. "And of course there's the money."

"Yeah. That helps." *To pay my college fees, my rent, my bus fares.*

"But!"

"Yeah—but!"

"Is it what you really want? To be the clothes *horse* rather than the clothes *designer*, the passive hook for someone else's creativity?"

Frankie shook her head. "I need to model to earn some cash.

But what I *want* to do is make jewelry." *Bangles and ankle bracelets, beads and belts, brooches, badges, buttons, and headbands.*

Once more Claudia chose to take her at her word. "Then you have to find a better balance between your modeling jobs and your work here," she pointed out. "Listen, I had to do it when I was your age. I had to pay my own way because back home in Austria my father was working as a garage mechanic and my mother was a school cook. They couldn't possibly afford to put me through college.

"I came over here and took a job as a waitress, knocking on the doors of big names like Asprey and Bulgari, trying to impress them with the originality of my designs. Eventually I squeezed in through the back door as a diamanteur with a Dutch diamond expert, fixing loose stones in antique jewelry, and then, when my boss began to trust my judgement, traveling to Angola to source stones for new designs."

Frankie listened hard. The thing that struck her was that Claudia had worked her way up from nothing. Now her designs were known all over the world and she taught in the top fashion college in Europe. "I guess I'm pretty feeble," she admitted. "I ought to give more attention to my work here."

"You're too easily sidetracked. That's nothing unusual. But the difficulty with you, Frankie, is that your confidence is easily dented. You need to grow a thicker skin and a bigger ego, otherwise knocking on doors and having them slammed in your face is going to hurt your self-esteem."

"You think I can do it?" God, how lame did that sound—as if she was begging for compliments!

Claudia tutted impatiently. "Come back in twenty-four hours with a fresh idea for your end-of-year show," she ordered. "Then I'll tell you whether or not you can succeed!"

"I need more space!" Marina told Tristan in words of one syllable.

She'd spent a whole hour trying to explain to her Head of Department why her shoe designs should not be crammed into an out of the way corner, but out in the center of the exhibition hall. They'd discussed the importance of shoes in setting the style for an entire collection, the fascinating history of shoes, the eclectic ethnicity of contemporary designs, the exquisite workmanship and quality materials that turned footwear into supreme objects of desire. Throughout it all, Tristan had skillfully avoided addressing Marina's complaint.

Now though, she had given it to him straight: "If I don't get more space for my shoes, I'll switch to Fine Art!"

Tristan gave a light cough, as if trying not to laugh. "Excuse me?"

"I will. I'm not kidding. Jack Irvine says I have talent!"

"Listen, you'll have to run this by me again. Are you telling me that old goat, Irvine, is trying to poach you from my fashion course?"

"I want my stuff to be valued," she explained. "If you stick my shoes in a corner, it feels like you don't think I'm any good."

"But, Marina, darling, everyone wants more space, better space, *all* the space!" Tristan ran a hand through his trendy, choppy haircut. "There's only so much I can allocate to each student."

"So who decides that Katrine Walker gets the display area that hits everyone smack between the eyes the second they walk into the room?"

"I do," Tristan admitted.

Marina frowned. "Okay, so what makes her knitwear more exciting and attention-grabbing than my shoes?" *Knitting's for grannies. I thought we were meant to be cutting edge.*

"Come!" Tristan instructed, wafting Marina along the corridor and upstairs to the textile workshop. They entered a huge room with high ceilings, where tall windows let in maximum daylight. Work benches ran the length of the studio, piled high with fabrics, sewing machines, boxes of threads, beads, and multicolored yarns. Tristan led her to a bench in the far corner. "This is what makes knitting exciting!" he said, in answer to her earlier question.

Marina took in Katrine's work-in-progress. There was a cropped, buttercup yellow knitted jacket with short sleeves, teamed with a long-sleeved cornflower blue cardigan. Beside these was a fabulous, fine-gauge purple ribbed sweater then a turquoise and chocolate gored skirt knitted in a soft cashmere and lambswool mix. The whole bench reminded her of a painter's palette—blue and yellow ochre, rusty reds, subtle browns, and greens.

"See?" Tristan said. "Knitwear isn't only for fuddy-duddies."

Sighing, Marina felt the texture of the garments. "They'll look great with big beads and armfuls of bangles."

"Katrine plans to display them on mannequins. They need plenty of space to set them off."

"Okay, I take your point." Marina knew there was no mileage in arguing anymore. She would have to make do with the titchy space she'd been given.

"And it's not to do with me thinking you're no good," Tristan assured her. "In fact, my opinion is that you do have what it takes."

"I do?" Marina didn't feel that Tristan was bullshitting. He wasn't the type.

He nodded. "You've come on in leaps and bounds this year. I like the way you've moved on from the ethnic phase, through eighties glam, into this understated elegance you're going for now."

"Yeah? I'm not sure. I'm sticking with the basic shapes of the fifties—but I wonder if I've given them enough of a contemporary edge."

"You have. Your colors sing, just like the colors in Katrine's work. Your attention to detail is strong."

"Cool." Marina looked for an escape route while she was winning. She found it in the opening of the workshop door and the entrance of Katrine herself, along with her best mate, Daisy Fenwick. "See you," she said swiftly to Tristan.

"Make the most of your space," he recommended. "Be ambitious with it. Sock the competition in the jaw!"

"Got it." Marina nodded at Katrine and Daisy, who both returned cheesy smiles.

"And tell Jack Irvine you're mine!" Tristan called after her. "And that you have way too much ambition to want to starve in a garret with a set of oil paints for company!"

Travis set up studio lights and worked out exposure times. He coped well with stuff that happened in a nanosecond, with the old-fashioned click of a shutter, like an infinitesimal blink of a lid across an eye. Anything with decimals or fractions he was fine with.

"What's wrong with Sinead?" Rob had asked him earlier that morning, as Travis had burned the toast and spilled hot coffee down his T-shirt.

"Don't know, mate." All he'd done was ask her if she wanted breakfast and she'd stormed off. She'd bumped into Rob on the way out of the house. "I think I mentioned the 'f' word."

Rob's eyebrows shot up, but he didn't comment.

"No, not what you're thinking! I mean the 'f' word, as in 'food.'"

Rob had grabbed a hunk of Travis's toast and smothered it with butter and marmalade. "What're you on about?"

"F-o-o-d. Sinead's got a phobia about eating. She won't touch anything that contains more than ten calories."

"Man, she'll waste away!"

Travis had nodded. "That's her plan."

And no, he didn't understand it. As he fixed lights and set up his tripod in the photography studio, he tried to work out how a girl as gorgeous as Sinead could possibly believe she needed to do more work on her appearance. "Look in the mirror, babe," he would say to her. "You're so beautiful!"

But she said she saw flab and massive thighs, she hated to look at herself.

"You're crazy," he wanted to say, but this would kick her off into another neurosis, how she knew she was too much like her mother, the original drama queen, how it was genetic and she knew she was going to turn out angst-ridden and unhappy, just like Daniella.

"Hey!" Sinead said now, coming into the studio. "Sorry about earlier."

"What?" Travis acted like he'd forgotten all about it. "Listen, babe, I need you to stand here while I angle the light properly. I'm setting everything up for the photo shoot."

Sinead went and stood patiently where she'd been told. She was pale and shaking slightly, after her walk from Walgrave Square into college. "I just saw Frankie," she told Travis. "Claudia gave her a hard time. Frankie has to start over with her jewelry designs." Which meant the no-eating thing might have to go on a day or two longer than Sinead had planned. "Can I sit down on that stool for a second?"

Travis looked up from his technical work and recognized the floaty, unfocused look on Sinead's face. He rushed for the stool and sat her down.

"You okay?" he asked anxiously.

She nodded. Wanting to deflect attention, she took a quick

swig of water from the bottle in her bag, then dug deeper into the bag for photographs of the body-art designs she'd worked on. "Tell me what you think of these and be straight with me, Travis. Don't say you like them just to be nice."

He studied the photos, noting how Sinead had worked with the curves of the body on the mannequin she'd practiced on. "They're going to look a bit like Maori tattoos," he remarked.

"Yeah, but they're not permanent, and that's part of what this is about. They'll be there for a while, then they'll start to fade and finally vanish completely. I like the idea that they're not there forever, that you're not stuck with them. You can change them, like you change your clothes."

"Yeah, I'm not into tattoos," Travis said.

"Frankie says now that she's ditched the enamel idea and that she wants to work some lapis lazuli into the jewelry she's designing."

"Lapis what?"

"Lazuli. It's a bright blue stone from the Himalayas or somewhere. Anyway, it reminds me of peacocks."

"Will it fit in with your body art?"

Sinead nodded. "Yeah, it'll bring a touch of exoticism. I think it'll work."

". . . *If!*" Travis cut in.

"If what?"

"If Frankie stops pissing around and gets her act together."

"Don't remind me!" Sinead groaned. After all the crises Sinead had been through with her mother and the house, and with the on-off nature of her relationship with Travis, it would be ironic if she failed her first year because of Frankie. "But hey, I know Frankie—she won't let me down."

Travis smiled briefly. "I've been editing the recordings I got of you and Marina and Frankie. Rob's found me some music for the sound track."

Sinead bristled. "Are you still planning to use it?"

"Only if you say yes. But if I don't go ahead, I fail my assessment. I'll have to re-take the year."

"No pressure there, then!" Sinead tried a feeble joke. No way did she want to wreck his chances, but on the other hand, she was still angry with him for filming them without explanation. "Can I look at it before I decide?"

"Can you look at it? Babe, if you want, you can help me *edit* it!"

She laughed. "I hope you got me on my good side."

"Do you have a bad side?"

"Yeah, this one!" She turned her right profile toward him. "See this bump on my nose?"

He didn't. "My God, the Elephant Man!"

Sinead hit out weakly and missed. "Stop it, I'm knackered!"

"I love you," he said suddenly.

"Me too," she replied. "Come on, let's go and have coffee."

"Look at this!" Frankie was excited as she showed Marina and Sinead her latest sketches. She'd worked like a maniac all day to get the designs to a stage where they were presentable. "This is a high collar of silver and lapis lazuli, with a matching bracelet that wraps around the upper arm, very Cleopatra!"

"Cool!" Marina murmured. Frankie's designs were simple and bold. The blue stone would zing out against Sinead's blond hair and pale, smooth skin.

"I like the asymmetry." Sinead considered the drawings more carefully. "And yeah, I think the color of the stone is going to work."

"What color tones will you use in your body art?" Marina wanted to know.

"Indigo, azure—lots of different shades of dark blue, merging into violet." Sinead's imagination got to work. Now that she saw what was in Frankie's head, she was prepared to rethink the designs she'd already developed. She began to draw deftly on the back of Frankie's sheets. "I can use shapes from Egyptian hieroglyphics—birds, snakes, and maybe other animals—like this."

Marina nodded. She flipped up the lid of her phone to read the message she'd just received from Rob.

`Am stil waiting 4 intervu. Guy is late`

`Stay calm. Gd luck`, she texted back. "Rob's radio guy is late," she reported. "That's probably a bad sign, isn't it?"

"How come?" Frankie asked. She was ready to head upstairs to her room to work through the night on a version of her designs that she could present to Claudia next morning.

"He's the producer. If he was really interested in giving Rob a job, he'd be on time for the interview, wouldn't he?"

"Not necessarily," Sinead argued. "Maybe the guy needs a new watch."

"Hmm. Rob wants this pretty bad."

"Well, I think he'll make a cool DJ," Frankie said as she dashed upstairs.

"Me too." Sinead got up to answer a ring on the doorbell. "Anyway, I'll say a little prayer."

"Right. That guarantees him the job, then." Marina grinned, trying to calm her own nerves. She pictured Rob at the radio station, dressed as always in his biker jacket and boots, trying to look laid-back with his right foot raised and resting on his left knee, tapping the side of his boot with his fingers, setting up a rhythm to a tune that would be playing inside his head.

Sinead opened the door to a woman in a dark gray suit, with her sleek brown hair lifted back from a carefully made-up face and swirled into a loose knot on top of her head. Beside her stood a kid of about fifteen, obviously her son, with the same straight nose and greenish gray eyes. "Yes?" she said abruptly, thinking that the visitors had come to the wrong house.

"Is Marina here?" the woman asked.

Sinead took a step back in surprise. "What? Oh yes. Marina, it's for you!" she yelled down the hallway, before backing quickly into the front lounge.

Putting Rob's impending interview to the back of her mind,

Marina went to the door. But she was still in a bit of a daze and the visitors stood with their backs to the light. There was a slight delay before she recognized them. "Mum! Tom!"

Sinead came back out of the lounge and walked up behind Marina. She smiled at the woman and boy. Their expressions were anxious; the kid hung back behind his mother.

"Can we come in?" Alice Kent asked.

Six

"Yes, come in!" Covering up for Marina's stunned silence, Sinead invited Marina's mother and brother into the lounge. "Sit down. Would you like a cup of coffee?"

"Thank you. You must be Sinead." Alice Kent managed some small talk, but the tight expression on her face conveyed the strain. "Sorry to land on you like this."

"No need to be sorry." Slipping quietly from the room, Sinead gave Marina's hand a quick squeeze.

"Where's Dad? What's happened?" Marina spoke for the first time. She had to sit down to hear the news.

"They can't find him," her mum said. "His phone's still dead. His firm has contacted the Niger government, and they've put him on a list of missing persons."

"Missing persons!" Marina echoed. It was official. "Oh my God!"

Her brother hung his head and stared at the floor.

"Okay, Marina, listen!" Alice Kent ploughed on through a

speech she'd obviously rehearsed. "It may not be as bad as it sounds. Communications are very poor in that part of Africa. Roads can get blocked by landslides; whole villages are cut off. It's possible your father has got caught up in some unreported natural disaster and in a few days he'll be back in touch."

"Coffee!" Sinead announced, reappearing with Frankie by her side. The tension in the room could be cut with a knife.

Marina shut her eyes and pursed her lips. "Missing!" she whispered again.

"We know he landed in Niger and met up at the airport with a government official and an Irish woman from Médecins Sans Frontières who were there to guide him around an area with a bad drought problem. Your father's job was to advise the government on how to bring a better water supply to the region."

"What happened after he left the airport?" Marina wanted to know. "Did anyone stay in contact with him?"

Her mother shook her head. "He didn't make his normal phone call to Head Office. And the MSF people haven't been able to get in touch with their woman either. The Niger government has got their official back, but he says he fixed up your father and the woman called Kim Cosgrove with a jeep then sent them off alone."

"Great!" Marina shook her head, taking coffee from Sinead and glancing at her brother, who sat hunched in the window seat. *My father is officially missing in a region where even a government employee refuses to set foot!* "What now?"

Her mother took a deep breath. "We wait," she said firmly. "And we don't panic."

Frankie's eyes were wide as she stole a glance at Sinead. Alice Kent was one self-controlled lady!

"Marina, we don't panic!" Alice repeated. "I've taken Tom out of school to come home and wait for news, but I want you to continue at college. This is too big a year for you to opt out of."

"What about Tom's exams?" Marina's head was spinning. She felt she wanted to go home and wait with them but knew that there was never any point in arguing with her mum.

"His GCSEs aren't until next year. The head teacher said the stress of waiting in school would be too much and recommended that Tom come back with me. I'm not sure they're right. But now, do you think *you* can cope?"

"I guess." Marina gave a helpless shrug. "How long will it be before they tell us anything?" *And who's "they"? Are "they" really taking this seriously? Is my dad ever going to come home?*

"Not long." For the first time her mother gave a vague answer and her calm expression gave way to panic. But she fought her fear and was quickly back in control. "I promise to let you know the moment we get any news."

"Why don't you stay here with us?" Sinead suggested. "At least for tonight."

"That's very kind, but no thanks." Alice stood up. "Now that I've picked Tom up and seen Marina face-to-face, I ought to get back home in case anyone needs to contact me."

"There's enough room here, honestly!"

"No . . . thanks."

"If you're sure . . ." Sinead gave up. How weird to have a mother like Alice, who coped with a major crisis by hiding her emotions and being totally practical. In this situation, Daniella would have been tearing out her hair.

"We'll look after Marina for you," Frankie promised, backing out of the way as Alice and Tom made for the door. "And Rob. He'll take care of her too."

Alice nodded. "She's lucky to have such good friends." She didn't linger to check that her daughter was okay, simply gave her a peck on the cheek and ushered Tom down the path. "I'll call soon," she promised.

Marina watched her mother and brother get into the car. She waved them off as if everything was normal. Then she went back inside, got as far as the bottom of the stairs, and broke down and cried her heart out.

"Hey!" Rob said. He held Marina in his arms.

Frankie had called him and he'd left the radio station without waiting for the producer to turn up. He'd roared into Walgrave Square on his Yamaha, sprinted up the path, and whisked Marina upstairs to her room.

"For a tough guy Rob can be really gentle," Frankie had commented wistfully.

"Yeah, he'd do anything for her," Sinead had agreed.

"Don't cry," he told Marina tenderly, sitting her on the bed and wiping away the tears. "From what you tell me, your dad can look after himself."

"That's not the point," she whispered. "This isn't like Boy Scouts getting lost in the Lake District, where you can call for a search party and it comes dashing up the mini-mountain. This is the middle of abso-bloody-lutely nowhere!"

"Wait. What do we actually know about the place?" Until now, Rob hadn't even heard of Niger. "Is it a war zone, or what?"

Marina shook her head. "I don't think so. I don't know."

"Let's take this a step at a time. For a start, your dad's company wouldn't send him somewhere where they were shooting and blowing each other up. I reckon he's driven off road and got lost. Or the jeep's broken down in the desert. In a day or two someone will find them and he'll be back in contact."

"Mum said there was an Irish woman with him." For a split second Marina had the crazy notion that her dad and this Kim Cosgrove had started a passionate affair and had deliberately lost themselves in the middle of Africa. But then she thought, *No, he wouldn't be that stupid. And anyway this is my dad we're talking about! My gray-haired, gray-suited, dead-sensible dad.*

"Try not to worry," Rob urged, his arms still around her, trying to imagine what it must be like to be driving through a dust storm in a parched landscape in baking heat, getting more and more lost, praying for a miracle.

*

"I don't know how Marina's going to concentrate on getting ready for the show now that this thing with her dad has kicked off," Frankie said.

She and Sinead were heading into college early next morning. It was a great day. The sun was shining. In the Square pink petals were fluttering down from the blossom trees like confetti.

Sinead agreed. "It's all she needs right now. By the way, when are you seeing Claudia?"

"Nine thirty. Jeez, I'm going to be late!" Checking her watch, Frankie broke into a run down Nugent Street. "Catch you on the flip!" she yelled.

"Yeah, meet me in the coffee bar at eleven!" Sinead refused to let on that she didn't have the energy to run with Frankie. Instead, she stopped in front of the window of Myers' Art Shop, pretending to be interested in the acrylic paints on offer to students at a 20 percent discount. Then she sat on a bench in a bus stop, took out her phone, found her mother's number, and called her. "Hi, Daniella. It's me."

"Darling. Lovely to hear your voice, but I'm in a bit of a rush."

"Sorry. But it's important."

There was a long pause. "I have to be somewhere by ten. But I can give you a couple of minutes. Go ahead."

"Daniella, who do you know who works in the Foreign Office?" Sinead asked. "Y'know, that guy who always sends you a case of wine for your birthday."

"What a strange question! Who do I know in the Foreign

Office?" Daniella sounded totally puzzled. "Oh, you must mean James Craven! He's a sweetie. Why, what about him?"

"How high up is he?"

"Scarily high, darling, considering our misspent youth. He's a Permanent Secretary. Listen, what has dear old Jamie Craven got to do with anything?"

Sinead knew her time was running out. She could picture her mother glancing at her watch, running a lipstick across her lips, getting ready to go out and meet whoever it was for coffee and chat. "I want you to call him," she told Daniella carefully.

"Whatever for?"

"You remember my housemate, Marina? . . . No, not Frankie. She's the dark one. Marina has long blond hair. Yes. Well, she needs someone with lots of influence to make some phone calls for her."

"Really? Whatever for?"

Sinead took a deep breath then forged ahead. "Her dad's gone missing in Niger."

"Oh darling, how awful! Tell me more!" Daniella gasped, prepared for once to delay going out and to listen in detail to what Sinead had to say.

"Well?" Sinead demanded as Frankie loped into the coffee bar and sat down opposite her.

Frankie raised her eyebrows and shrugged.

"Come on, what did Claudia say?"

In the past hour since she'd spoken to her mother, Sinead had gone looking for Tristan Fox and found him in his office. She'd explained Marina's family crisis and asked if there was any way Marina could be let off her end-of-year assessment.

"How is she coping?" Tristan had responded. "Is she managing to hold herself together?"

Sinead had shaken her head. "She didn't sleep all last night. Her boyfriend's with her right now. They're waiting for news."

The Head of Department had made a big deal of what would happen if Marina missed the show. "She's a good student. Her work has great flair. But unless she has something concrete to show for her year's work, her grades will suffer."

"That's so mean!" Sinead had protested. This was where she'd hoped her mother's contacts might come in useful again. After all, Daniella and Tristan also went way back to shared and misspent youths. So Sinead had been able to come on strong in a way that other students would never have dared. "You could let Marina off the hook if you wanted," she'd insisted. "There must be a way of still awarding her a good grade."

Tristan had sat for ages, trying to dodge a plain answer, but Sinead hadn't let him. "Tell her to come and see me," he'd said finally, and, more or less satisfied with this, Sinead had fled before he changed his mind.

Now Frankie sat down for coffee and looked hard at Sinead. There was something different about her but Frankie couldn't exactly say what it was. Maybe a bit more color in her face and life in her eyes. Oh, and was that a half-eaten chocolate brownie on a plate in front of her? *Good Christ!* Frankie practically fell off her seat. "Claudia said yes," she muttered slowly, unable to take her eyes off the heap of yummy, dark brown calories.

"Cool!" Sinead said, biting deep into the brownie then carelessly swallowing it down with a mouthful of cappuccino. "Okay, Frankie, you got the thumbs-up from the pint-sized prima donna. Now, all we have to do is get our act together!"

"Yeah," Frankie stammered, *Au revoir, anorexia. 'Allo, gateau!*

Sinead didn't even seem to notice. "Cool. I'll start mixing the dyes, while you switch on that old stone polisher and get grinding lapis lazuli until it shines like the Aegean Sea!"

Sorry, can't do it. Frankie texted a reply to the Bed-Head office. She'd had a message asking if she could jump on the train to Edinburgh and do a shoot for the Scottish Tourist Board. Am busy until end of month.

Did I really just do that? she asked herself. She practically saw the twenty-pound notes fluttering away like blossom petals from the cherry trees earlier that day. But the recent interview with Claudia was still fresh in her mind and she was dead set on proving that she was worth the tutor's faith in her.

"This is going to be the best!" she said out loud. In the background the engine of the polisher hummed and the stones inside the tiny drum rattled.

"Hey, Frankie, you know what they say!" Travis cut in.

She looked up over the rim of her goggles. "No, I don't, Trav, but I expect you're going to tell me!"

"Talking to yourself is the first sign of madness."

"Listen, I'm the only person round here who I can have a decent conversation with!" she joked. Poor Marina was still at home in pieces. Sinead was babbling on about her mother and some guy called James Craven. That was two reasons why Frankie had escaped back to college and the jewelry workshop this late in the evening.

"I'm meeting up with Lee in the bar, if you fancy joining us," Travis told her before he sauntered on.

She didn't, so she stayed and worked instead.

"So anyway, Rob could have missed out on the biggest career opportunity of his life!" Travis told Lee, who was a mate from the Moving Images course. They'd talked for a while about the projects they were putting finishing touches to, then moved on to Rob and the radio producer.

Lee drank from his bottle then shook his head. "I know how much Rob must've wanted that," he grunted. "Did the guy try to get in touch to find out why Rob didn't show?"

"Dunno." Travis reflected on the past few days. "It's been a roller coaster," he admitted. "Rob nearly gets his biggest break, then he doesn't. I almost have to ditch my documentary, then suddenly it's back on. Sinead half starves herself for more than a week, but now she can't keep off the Big Macs!"

"Women!" Lee interrupted with the usual corny comment. "Hey, I heard Frankie's boycotting the end-of-year show."

"*Was!*" Travis corrected. "She did a kamikaze act, then pulled herself out of it at the last minute. Now she's working like a crazy woman. I just left her in the workshop, soldering and polishing."

Lee nodded. "So she'll be here in college next year?"

"Dunno, mate." Travis shrugged. "Maybe the modeling will take off big style."

Leaving Lee to brood over this, Travis got up to go to the Gents. He was only gone two minutes, but when he got back, Lee's place at the bar was empty.

Frankie loved the precision of working with precious metals and stones. Though the rest of her life was lived in a mad rush, with jeans, shirts, skirts, and boots spilling out of her wardrobe, and never enough floor space in her room to run a Hoover around, she did have this calm oasis of the workshop where every tiny object had its place, and order reigned. And, pow!—the end result was sheer beauty.

She worked on without looking at the clock, measuring then setting oblong pieces of lapis lazuli into silver frames, before attaching each one to a moulded circlet of silver that would sit around Sinead's neck and rest just above the collarbones. Only when she had finished setting the stones did she stand back and raise her goggles.

"Hey, Frankie," Lee said quietly.

She jumped sideways and gasped.

"Travis said you were here."

Thanks, Trav! Frankie guessed that Velcro Boy had come up here straight from the bar. She could smell beer on his breath inside the small room. How come his shirts were always so neatly pressed? Did he have an iron on constant standby? "I'm busy, Lee," she said.

"I thought you might want to come down for a drink."

"No, thanks."

Lee swallowed his disappointment and switched tactics. "I heard about Marina's dad."

"Yeah, it sucks." Thinking that if she lowered her goggles, Lee would take the hint, Frankie got busy again.

"Is there any news?"

"No."

How could a girl in goggles still look sexy? Lee wondered. He knew the beer had got to his brain, that he probably wasn't judging things well, but he blundered on. "It got onto the local news."

"What did?"

"Martin Kent going missing. They interviewed a guy from his water company."

Once more, Frankie raised her goggles. "What did he say?"

"They're doing everything possible blah-blah. Then a Foreign Office bloke came on to describe the situation in Niger."

At this, Frankie pricked up her ears. "What was his name?"

"John—James something."

". . . Craven!" Frankie gasped. *Result!* Trust Sinead and Daniella to get things moving! "Tell me more!" she begged Lee. "Come on, what are we waiting for? You've got to buy me that drink!"

Seven

On Tuesday night hopes were raised.

Sitting with Rob in the front room at Number 13, Marina heard a news broadcast and the interview with James Craven. His calm assessment of her dad's plight helped settle her nerves.

"The political situation out there is stable," he'd told the reporter. "There is enormous poverty and the infrastructure is underdeveloped, but at present we don't suspect sinister cause for Mr. Kent's disappearance."

"What does that mean?" Marina asked Rob.

"The roads are bad, but no one's shooting the crap out of anyone else."

"So they don't think he's been kidnapped?" This was one of Marina's worst fears. A hostage situation could go on for months, even years. Usually the western government refused to pay a ransom or give in to any of the hostage takers' demands.

"The guy more or less said it was the rough terrain that's responsible for your dad's disappearance." Rob did his best to reassure her. "Don't worry, there'll be people looking for him—helicopters and so on. It won't be long now."

On Wednesday morning, Marina decided to drag herself into college.

"Take her on the bike," Frankie suggested to Rob. "Make sure she gets there and doesn't chicken out."

"Yeah, it'll help take her mind off things," Sinead agreed. She'd been on the phone again to Daniella, pestering her to keep in touch with her Foreign Office buddy.

By ten o"clock, Marina was walking with Rob through the main entrance, feeling as if the whole world was staring at her.

There's the kid whose dad has disappeared! How tragic is that! But how come she's still here? Why hasn't the whole family flown out to look for him?

"Hi, Marina!" Suzy Atkins called across the entrance hall. "Any news?"

Marina shook her head. "I'm boiling!" she sighed, unzipping her jacket and loosening her hair.

"Give me your helmet," Rob offered.

"Sorry to hear about your dad!" Lee Wright told her as he passed them in the corridor.

"Marina, good to see you!" Tristan came out of his office to greet her. "I heard what happened. Why not come in and have a chat?"

Rob gave her a small shove from behind, and before she knew it she was inside the Head of Department's room.

The office was light, the window open. The off-white walls were lined with elegant architectural prints of the Duomo in Florence and St. Peter's in Rome. Tristan's vast glass desk filled half of the floor space.

"Sit," he told her.

Marina's head was spinning as she sank onto a chrome and white leather chair. Tristan's face was blurred.

"I sympathize with what you must be going through," he began formally. "I expect the time is dragging. Every minute must feel like an hour."

She nodded.

"How's your mother doing?"

"She's good. She says not to panic."

"Exactly. But I expect that's easier said than done."

Marina frowned. Tristan was being kinder than she'd expected. "I haven't been able to do much work," she stammered.

"No. Sinead told me. But listen, you have ten whole days before the show. Even if you don't hear anything from Niger before the weekend, and say things worked out by Saturday or Sunday, you would still have time to pull it together. And you made it here today," he pointed out.

But my head's a mess, my heart's racing, and I feel sick! Sitting there in the beautiful minimalist space, Marina felt a sudden urge to run home to Walgrave Square.

"If the worst comes to the worst, and you can't finish your project, we can accept a note from your GP citing stress as a reason for your withdrawal," Tristan explained.

A sickie. A blank space in the exhibition hall where my shoe designs should be! Marina swallowed hard.

"We wouldn't ask you to repeat a year, or anything nasty like that."

She nodded. "Thanks, but I want to complete my project," she insisted quietly.

Tristan took a long look at her strained, pale face, then nodded. "Good." He got up from his chair and stood by the window overlooking the busy street. "By the way," he said, hands in pockets, staring out at the buses, trucks, and cars, "I've got you a summer placement with Charles Jourdan."

"That's like saying Dior or Chanel!" Marina explained to Rob about her work experience. "Charles Jourdan is the Yves Saint Laurent of shoes!"

"That's cool, babe." Rob was picking up a message on his phone, surrounded by debris from takeaway meals and empty cans in his and Travis's living room at Number 45.

Marina had spent all day at college completing a new design for purple snakeskin shoes. They were slingbacks with an inch platform and a four-inch, tapering heel. Pink piping and a neat bow completed the vintage effect. She'd been so into her work that for five whole minutes that afternoon she'd managed to push her dad's plight right out of her mind.

Now though, her mood had taken a dive and she needed Rob's reassurance, so she'd rushed back to his place and told him about her summer placement.

"Tristan designs for Jourdan, so that's how come he managed to get me a placement," she explained.

Rob was distracted by his message.

"Bad news?" Marina asked. A shudder ran through her. Maybe Sinead or Frankie had taken a call and got in touch with Rob so that he could prepare her for the worst. "Is it Dad?"

"No, just some work stuff." Chucking his phone onto the sofa, he cuddled up beside Marina. "So when does this dream placement kick off?" he wanted to know.

"End of June. What work stuff?" Marina could tell when Rob was blowing her off. He usually got physical and crowded in on her.

"Nothing. I'll tell you later. Do you want a drink?"

"No. Yes, coffee, please." She'd changed her mind so that he would have to go into the kitchen and she would sneak a quick look at his phone. She picked it up from under a cushion, pressed "Menu" then "Short Messages," then scrolled down to "Inbox" and selected the latest number.

Tim Yorke wants 2 c u Fri am, she read.

Marina yelped, jumped up, and ran into the kitchen. "Who's Tim Yorke?" she demanded. "Is he the guy from the radio?"

Rob stood, coffee spoon raised, ready to tip the granules into the mug. "You read my message!" he accused.

"Yeah, sorry. I didn't believe you—I thought it might really be about Dad." Marina grabbed his arm. The coffee powder spilled everywhere. "So, is Tim Yorke the radio guy?"

"You've got no shame. Yeah, he is." Rob blushed as he scraped up the mess and poured hot water into the mug.

"Rob, this is so cool!" Marina squealed. "You should've told me."

"It might not work out," he told her. "Keep the noise down. You'll upset the old biddy next door."

"You're gonna be a radio DJ!" she cried, flinging her arms around him and throwing him off balance.

Coffee slopped onto the worktop and trickled down the front of the unit. Marina kissed Rob and he kissed her back.

Frankie and Sinead worked all through Wednesday and Thursday to be ready for the photo shoot on Thursday evening. At 6:00 p.m. Frankie's jewelry still wasn't finished, but Travis went ahead and worked on the studio lights, helped by Lee.

"Frankie's panicking," Travis reported. "She's in the workshop with smoke practically coming out of her ears."

Lee fixed cable to the floor with gaffer tape. "Where's Sinead?"

"In the life-drawing studio, painting patterns on her body. Man, talk about uptight!"

Lee sucked through his teeth as if he knew exactly where Travis was coming from. "It's a big thing, this end-of-year show. I guess you can understand why the girls are so stressed."

"Just don't get in their way for the next couple of hours." Travis checked settings on his SLR camera, which he still preferred to digital. "In fact, Lee, if you're planning to stick around for the shoot, I'd advise no talking, no moving, no breathing."

"I'm out of here," Lee said hastily, but not quickly enough, because he bumped into Frankie on his way out.

"Lee!" she cried, shoving her bare arm into his face. "What does this arm band look like? Is it straight, or do the stones drag it down at one side?"

The arm looked fine to Lee—tanned, smooth, and totally desirable. "It seems good to me," he muttered.

"And what about the collar? Does it stand up at the back when I move, or does it rest on the nape of my neck?" She held up her long, dark hair for him to see.

He tried to figure out the right answer, but lust blinded him. Frankie's neck was long and slender. Little wisps of hair curled over the silver collar.

"Anyhow, it's too late now!" Frankie decided, not waiting for an answer and rushing on into the studio. "Hey, Travis, isn't this excite-tastic!"

"This is doing my head in!" he countered. "I've checked everything three times, and I know nothing's going to go wrong, but my nerves feel as if they've been through the shredder!"

Frankie unclasped the arm band and loosened the collar from her neck. "Where's Sinead?"

"Panicking in the life-drawing studio. No, here she is." Travis stood aside to avoid the sudden swing of the opening door. Sinead joined them, covered from head to toe in a pale blue Chinese silk dressing-gown, which she held clutched to her throat.

Frankie drew her between the studio lights and white screens into the center of the room. "Okay, let's take a look!"

"Oh God!" Sinead took a deep breath and froze. Suddenly this body-art-as-fashion statement didn't seem like such a good idea. "Frankie, I've changed my mind! Maybe we should get a life-drawing model instead!"

"Where do we magic one of them from? Look, we're all ready to go!" Frankie showed her the jewelry and pointed to the lights. "Sinead, you can't back out now!"

"*You* model them!" Sinead begged. "You're used to posing for the camera."

Frankie backed away. "Not without my clothes, I'm not!"

Sinead kept her dressing-gown closed to the neck. "What if it looks—tacky?"

"You mean, tacky as in pornographic? It won't. Not the way Travis lights it and takes the pictures. It'll look artistic and tasteful, won't it, Trav?"

"Can I wear a bikini?" Sinead's heart was racing; she would do anything to delay taking her robe off.

"Keep your knickers on but no top," Frankie insisted. "Look, it's only me and Travis you have to worry about, no one else will see anything and well, we've . . . we've . . ." Frankie spread both hands, palms up ". . . seen it all before!"

The look on Frankie's face made Travis break out into a laugh. Suddenly the nerves and the tension evaporated. Sinead joined in the laughter then began to explain how hard it had been to paint the patterns onto her body while looking in a mirror. "I had to treat my skin as a blank canvas and then do everything in reverse or upside down. It's probably a total mess."

"Show!" Frankie demanded. "Let's see what it looks like with my jewelry."

As Sinead finally let go of the dressing-gown, Frankie fastened the collar around her neck. For a second, neither Frankie nor Travis said a word.

"What do you think?" Sinead asked nervously. "Does it need more pattern on the shoulder, or is this enough?"

"Enough," Frankie said. The effect of the paint and jewelry combined was total knockout—exotic, graceful, rich, and unique.

"Tilt your chin upward," Travis told Sinead as he raised his camera and peered through the viewfinder. "Look slightly away toward the screen. Now bring your right arm across your body—a bit more—yeah, perfect!"

The camera clicked. Sinead and Frankie relaxed. Everything came good.

"We all went for a drink afterward," Sinead was telling Marina.

The photo session had gone like a dream. Frankie had taken shots on her digital camera while Travis worked on old-fashioned film. The digital shots were already downloaded and printed off from Sinead's computer, and she had shown them to Marina. "Look at these," she'd said, shoving the prints under Marina's nose over coffee in the house next morning. "Look at the lighting. Isn't it perfect?"

Marina had torn her thoughts away from her missing dad long

enough to view the photos. "Babe, you look stunning!" Sinead's body was sleek and sculptured, like marble. Travis had shot her against a pure white background, making Sinead's skinny, angular body almost fade into it, with no strong shadows, so that the eye was drawn to the body art and to Frankie's fantastic lapis lazuli stones.

"I don't look fat?" Sinead had checked, tipping into guilt over the brownies and Big Macs of the past few days.

Marina had raised her eyebrows. "No. You're skinny-tastic, as Frankie would say!"

Then Sinead mentioned the celebration. "We went to Escape, hoping to find you and Rob, but you weren't there."

"I was at his place." Still waiting for news. She'd stayed over at Number 45 and early this morning Rob had set off for his interview with Tim Yorke.

"When I say 'we,' I mean me, Frankie, Rob, and Lee," Sinead explained carefully.

"Lee?" Marina choked on her coffee. "Whose idea was that?"

"Frankie's. We bumped into him in the college bar and she invited him to Escape." Sinead grinned. "I know. Who'd have thought it!"

"Is that my phone?" Marina jumped again at a muffled ring tone.

"No, it's mine." Sinead fished in her bag, but before she found her phone, it went dead. "It's Daniella," she muttered, checking the missed call. "I'll call back later. Yeah, anyway, Frankie was actually being nice to Lee. I don't think he could believe it, judging by the stunned, am-I-dreaming look in his eyes." Again her phone went off and this time she got the call.

"Hi, Daniella. Yes, I'm at home. Yep, she's here. Do you want to speak to her?"

Marina's hand shook as she took Sinead's phone. "Hi, Mrs. Harcourt."

"Hello, Marina. Listen, darling, I wanted to bring you up to speed."

"Why, what's happened?" It must be bad news! She gripped the phone hard.

"I've just been speaking to Jamie Craven. It's all unofficial at the moment, but it seems that they've found your father."

Marina's throat went dry. She could hardly speak. "Is he okay?"

"By all accounts, he's alive and safe," Daniella reported. "I don't have any details, but the Foreign Office has had information from a source in Niger that two missing persons—a man and a woman—have been tracked down in a village a hundred miles north of the capital. Both are well."

Tears sprang to Marina's eyes. "Thank God!"

"Listen. Jamie says the news has still to be confirmed. That might take another twenty-four hours. But he assures me that a team of people from Médecins Sans Frontières have made contact with their worker and your father. They have to be brought out on foot for some reason that I don't understand. However, to cut a long story short, you should be able to speak to your father before the weekend."

"Thank you!" Marina whispered, passing the phone back to Sinead before it slipped from her trembling fingers.

"Look after her," Daniella told Sinead. "The poor darling must be traumatized."

"You're amazing," Sinead said to her mother. "I don't know how you do it, but you are—totally amazing!"

"I know the right people, that's all."

"Can Marina tell her mum?"

"Of course. But stress that the news won't become official until tomorrow, so they shouldn't expect any communication from London today. I'll text you Jamie's private number, so that Marina's mother . . ."

"Alice."

"Yes, Alice can talk to him direct. He's very good in that way—not at all stiff and starchy, as you might expect. Now, darling, I must run!"

Click. Sinead had no more time for gratitude. "She's gone," she told Marina gently.

Marina wiped her tears. "He's okay," she whispered. A weight had been lifted. That's what everyone said about the feeling of relief, and it was totally true.

"Don't cry."

"I'm not. I'm happy."

"Here, have a tissue."

"Where's my phone? I have to tell Mum."

Sinead held her hand to steady her. "Just think," she said. "This time tomorrow, your dad could be on his way home!"

Eight

"Prada Princesses: The Final Cut!" Travis announced, faking an American voice-over.

Sinead screwed up her mouth. "What do you mean, Prada Princesses? Are you saying that we're high maintenance—me, Frankie, and Marina?"

He backed off, defending himself with upraised hands. "Would I?"

"Listen to me, mister—we're just ordinary, common, or garden girls! We love shopping and getting ready to party. No way are we hard to please!"

Though it was Friday night they'd decided to stay in to view Travis's documentary. He'd downloaded the material from his camcorder onto disk, and now he wanted to show Sinead what he'd achieved with his brand-new editing program.

"Did I say you were?" he grinned, busy with his keyboard and mouse.

"That's what you meant." That they were spoiled little fashion victims, or else extravagant prima donnas. Perhaps both.

"Babe, I only meant you were drop-dead gorgeous." He was glad they were back to joking and exchanging insults rather than angst and arguments. Until the next time.

"Yeah, but I bet you've made us look hideous on this thing." Leaning over his shoulder, Sinead watched the title sequence come up on screen—more music video than reality TV. To a backing of rock music, she saw shots of herself staring straight at the camera, gray eyes wide, mouth half open, of Frankie grinning in the way that suggested that everything in life was a huge joke. Then there was Marina doing a Marilyn pose, hands on curvy hips, lips pouting. Travis had captured them at their best, then cut into it with black-and-white glimpses of Sinead putting on her makeup, Frankie emerging from under her duvet, bleary-eyed, Marina in the rain with helmet-hair, dashing across the pavement in her leathers.

"What's this music?" Sinead asked.

"A track from Bad Mouth—Rob's band. He suggested it."

"I know who Bad Mouth is," she protested, remembering a brief encounter she'd had with the singer after she and Travis had had one of their arguments.

"*Pretty on the outside, playin' to the crowd,*" Boz sang. "*All alone and fakin' it, now you ain't so proud.*"

"Thanks!" Sinead frowned. In spite of herself, she soon dropped the sarcasm and got drawn in. Travis had worked on a technique of slowing down a sequence to slow motion and standstill, then jerking it forward again as if she or Marina or Frankie were moving like puppets, or like figures in a silent movie. She didn't know how he'd done it, but it was cool. And the music echoed the fractured quality of the filming.

"Pretty on the outside, hey it's such a shame. All alone and fakin' it, babe, you are to blame."

"Look at this!" Travis froze the picture and pointed to a close-up of Sinead, eyes narrowed, wearing a wide blue bandana low over her forehead, looking like a suspicious warrior-woman from another continent, another century. "That's my favorite shot!"

She nodded. As Travis unfroze the picture and went on to show supermodel Frankie doing a big fashion shoot, with inset clips of her yawning and making black coffee in a cracked mug, or Marina slobbing in jogging pants in front of TV, Sinead had to admire what his prying camera had done. "It's a great sound track," she admitted. The words, "pretty on the outside," kept repeating and reinforcing the glamour shots, while all the stuff about being sad and lonely echoed the lost moments when the girls had been off guard.

"Do you like it?" Travis asked when the music and images had faded. "I can still change it some more if you want me to."

Sinead perched on the edge of his chair. "I never did like my nose!" she sighed. "But now I've watched this, I hate every part of my face—eyes, mouth—everything!"

"So you *don't* like it?"

"Frankie looks fantastic on the catwalk," she sighed. "And Marina's eyes are an amazing blue-green, like the ocean!"

Travis waited with a sense of doom. Sinead hated it. She was about to call him a voyeur and make him ditch the whole project! His budding career lay in ruins.

There was a pause that seemed to go on forever. Then Sinead leaned in for a full-on kiss. "You're a photographic genius!" she whispered. "The whole piece is amazing."

"Do you mean that?"

She nodded and kissed him again, murmuring with her soft lips against his, "Quentin Tarantino had better watch out!"

With hindsight, Marina realized that roaring up to her mum's quiet suburban house on Rob's 750cc motorbike had not been a good idea.

Come to think of it, going home at all, by any form of transport, seemed pretty dumb, now that they were here.

"Mum, you remember Rob?" Marina shoved an uneasy boyfriend over the Kent family threshold.

Alice and Rob politely shook hands. "I wasn't expecting you," Alice told Marina coolly.

"You talked to the Foreign Office guy, didn't you?" What was going on here? Why wasn't her mum smiling?

"Yes, I spoke to James Craven. He confirmed what you told me."

Marina turned to her brother, who was standing adrift from her, Rob, and their mother on the landing halfway up the stairs. "Isn't it cool that Dad's safe, Tom?"

"When will he be home?" he asked in that grunting, unemotional teenage tone that Marina had grown to expect.

"Soon. First they have to get him back to civilization. Then I expect he'll call us—maybe tomorrow."

"Have you eaten?" Alice asked.

"No, we dropped everything and shot up here on the bike," Marina answered. Rob had gotten back from his interview with Tim Yorke at midday and she'd immediately told him the good news about her dad. It had been his idea to visit.

"Babe, that's a big relief!" he'd said, lifting her off the ground in one of his bear hugs.

"How did the interview go?" she'd asked.

"Don't know. Seemed okay," was all he would say. Then, "Let's go visit your mum and kid brother. We can all go out for a meal to celebrate."

But, after their two-hour ride on the bike, it seemed Alice wasn't in the mood. "I can get a pizza out of the deep freeze," she said briskly. "Will you two want to stay the night?"

Marina stepped in quickly. "No, we only came on a flying visit. Did you get any more details out of Mr. Craven? Did he say exactly where they'd found Dad and why he went missing in the first place?"

"Only the basic facts." Alice Kent went through the motions of unwrapping the pizza to let it defrost. "I thought from the beginning that your father's company was overreacting. I knew it wouldn't be long before he turned up."

Behind Alice's back, Rob gave Marina a puzzled, how-come-she's-being-like-this glance.

"It was ridiculous to have him listed as officially missing and cause all that fuss. It meant bringing Tom out of school for a start. And I did tell you, Marina, to stay in college. You have so little time left before your assessment."

"I know, but I thought—*we* thought that we could maybe go out for a drink, or a meal, or something." Her mother's coolness was making Marina feel like someone had delivered a hefty kick to her stomach. "You *are* pleased he's been found, aren't you?"

"Of course I'm pleased. Tom, will you set the table in the dining room with place mats, knives, and forks? Rob, why don't you come and sit down in the lounge where it's more comfortable."

Rob glanced down at his boots. He took them off and left them looking huge and out of place in the hallway then followed Alice into a light room with two large sofas and a bay window overlooking a long, neat garden. He smiled uneasily, glad when Alice left him alone in the room.

So, how come? he thought. How come Marina's mum was playing the Ice Queen? And how did the gorgeous, sexy girl he'd fallen for slot into this prime example of middle-class uptightness? Even the purple tulips in the glass vase on the coffee table were standing to attention, for Christ's sake!

"How could you?" Alice Kent hissed at Marina as she cornered her in the kitchen, relieved Tom of his table-laying duties, and sent him upstairs to his room.

"What? What did I do?" Marina backed off, wondering if she'd lost a vital piece of the jigsaw without even noticing.

"How could you ditch all your college responsibilities and come flying up here on that ridiculous machine?" Alice's face was white and tight with anger. "In spite of what I said!"

Marina dug in her heels. "What's ridiculous about Rob's Yamaha?"

"You in those leather trousers and helmet for a start!" Wrenching open the oven door, her mother shoved the pizza inside and slammed the door. "You look like a Hell's Angel! And what about your end-of-year assessment?"

Finally Marina had had enough. "Okay, that's it!" she stormed. "I'm eighteen. You don't run my life anymore!"

As always, Alice quickly resorted to sarcasm. "Oh, no? Forgive me, Marina, but I thought I was paying your college fees and accommodation expenses. If that's not running your life, it is at least funding it."

"Jeez!" Marina let out an exasperated groan. "Anyone else would be happy when her husband showed up after he went missing in the middle of Africa. But not you, Mum. No, you look like you're sucking on a lemon as usual!"

"Is everything okay?" Rob stuck his head around the door. He'd picked up the raised voices and come to give Marina some support.

"Yeah, everything's cool, just as soon as we get out of here!" Marina cried. "Come on, Rob, I don't know why we bothered coming in the first place!"

He paused for a second to take in the scene—Marina's face hot and flushed, her hands trembling, Alice standing calmly by the oven, totally unmoved.

"Let's go," he agreed.

Five minutes later, they were zipped up inside their leathers, thrashing down the motorway as fast as the speed limit and 750 ccs of internal combustion engine would allow.

Six days and counting! Frankie tore the top leaf off her calendar, wishing that she hadn't just given way to pressure from Jessica West, the head of the Bed-Head agency, to slot in another last-minute shoot.

"I'd advise you to take it," Jessica had said on the phone. "It won't do you any good if you go off the map until you've finished your jewelry course. People in this industry have very short memories."

"When?" Frankie had asked.

"Tomorrow."

"Tomorrow's Sunday!"

"Yes. You'll be modeling beachwear. Have a session on the sunbed then get yourself out to Cromer by midday."

"Where's Cromer?"

"East coast somewhere. Look at a map."

"Fine," Frankie had sighed.

Other models went to Barbados, where the sand was white and the sea was blue. But not Frankie. No, she would have to shiver on a windy British beach, covered in goose pimples, trying to look sexy in a skimpy bikini. Still, it would put money in the bank.

*

"Daniella's treat," Sinead told Frankie and Marina as they booked in for a pamper session on Saturday afternoon. "She thinks poor Marina is in desperate need of a Thai massage!"

"Cool!" Frankie cried. "I get to top up my tan. What are you going to have, Sinead?"

"The works." Jacuzzi, sauna, exfoliating massage, leg wax, aromatherapy, and every kind of detox they could throw at her.

"I'm not sure I want to go right now!" Marina sighed. Since the abortive visit to her mum, she'd heard nothing. No one was telling her anything about when her dad would be back, and until she actually set eyes on him, she was living in limbo.

"Cheer up," Frankie urged. "You can have your nails done and get a facial. What more can any girl want?"

Marina smiled and nodded. "Okay. Where is this pamper place?"

"In town, on Britten Road." Sinead led the way. "Shall we call a cab?"

"What, you think we're all made of dosh like you?" Frankie protested, dragging Marina out of the house. "It's not far. We can walk."

Sinead looked at her as if she was mad.

"Horrible four-letter word—w-a-l-k!" Frankie insisted. "Fresh air. Exercise."

Setting off across the Square, they waved at Rob who was examining the oily innards of his bike engine, spanners in hand.

"Tell Travis I'll see him at eight!" Sinead called. She was looking forward to their unexpected girly treat, courtesy of her mother.

"Are you coming to see the show on Friday?" she'd asked, after she'd listened to Daniella's account of her latest conquest (loaded, polo-playing Argentinian named Bruno) and she'd at last been able to get a word in edgeways.

"What show?" her mother had asked.

"You know, our end-of-year show. Next Friday."

"Sorry, darling, I can't make Friday."

"That's okay, no problem."

"Maybe next year," Daniella had said then jumped in with a generous suggestion. "Sinead, why don't you and your house-mates spend the afternoon de-stressing? I have an account with a chain of beauty therapy centers. There's bound to be a branch near you."

And now here they were, the three of them, swanning into a swish place specializing in aromatherapy techniques, staffed by women in lilac, clinical-style overalls, carrying stacks of pristine white towels and pushing trolleys past steam rooms and spa baths. Marina, Frankie, and Sinead were whisked into a warm changing room and told to put on thick white dressing-gowns.

"How cool is this!" Frankie giggled, sliding her feet into a pair of brand-new toweling slippers.

"How much is this lot going to cost?" Marina gasped, pinning up her long hair.

A woman came, took them into a treatment room, and showed them how to step inside their own personal sauna box.

Sinead was the first victim. She took off her robe and sat on a ledge inside the dome-shaped box. A door closed around her, leaving only her head in view through a hole in the top. Then steam was pumped in through internal vents.

"Help, they're broiling Sinead!" Frankie cried. She watched the same thing happen to Marina. Then, when it was her turn, she sat obediently and felt the door click. Relaxing steam began to seep into her skin.

"Twenty minutes," their assistant said, leaving them to stew in peace.

"Can this be good for you?" Marina felt sweat trickling down her brow. "What happens if we get too hot?"

"Wimp," Sinead murmured, settling straight into the ethos that you had to suffer to be beautiful. "Just wait until they do the deep tissue massage—that really does kill!"

"Weird," Frankie mused, watching the soft-shoed masseuses come and go along the corridor. "In the middle ages this would have been a form of torture!"

"When will the twenty minutes be up?" Marina wailed.

From the steam boxes the girls leaped into a cold plunge pool and then into the jacuzzi.

"My skin feels squeaky clean!" Sinead sighed, leaving the jacuzzi and padding barefoot down the corridor to a room where a woman was heating flat, smooth stones, ready to lay them along Sinead's spine.

"Where's the sunbed?" Frankie asked another assistant, already feeling like a lobster must feel on his way to becoming thermidor.

Meanwhile, Marina opted for the Thai massage that Daniella had suggested. She lay on a high table in a room lit with candles and scented with jasmine. The masseuse gently placed white towels over her body. Marina closed her eyes.

"I was purring like a cat at the end of it," Marina told Sinead and Frankie. "One minute she was at my head, massaging my neck and shoulders. Next second she was down by my feet and I didn't even know she'd moved. It was as if she were floating!"

They'd met up between treatments in a big conservatory extension where they were made to drink cold fruit juices.

"So you feel better?" Sinead grinned. "Did you sense all the stress melting away?"

"Yes, really!" Marina enthused. "I never expected it to be this good." She thought for a while then laughed. "Maybe I should send my mother to one of these places!"

Frankie and Sinead waited for more. All they knew about yesterday was that Rob had taken Marina home to share the good news with her mother and brother, and that a dis-chuffed Mrs. Kent had more or less slammed the door in their faces.

"Rob was so-oh pissed off," Marina sighed. "I thought he was going to have a row right there and then. Luckily, I got him on the bike and we drove away before he could kick off."

"What's going on?" Frankie asked. "Is your mother always like this?"

"You mean, an uptight and miserable prune-face?" Marina gave a hollow laugh. "Yeah, pretty much." The rules had always been strict, all the time Marina was growing up—be quiet, be clean, don't speak until you're spoken to. "But I think she's gotten worse lately."

"If your mother's so mean, how come you're so . . ." Sinead searched for the right word and came up with the obvious ". . . kind?"

"Am I?" Marina smiled back over the top of her glass of tomato juice.

"Big time!" Frankie assured her. Marina was always the one who jumped in to help when anyone was in trouble. And she'd been a good mate to Frankie during the nightmare time with Wim van Bulow, Frankie's two-timing Juggler Man. "We can rely on you."

"You can?"

Sinead nodded. "You must take after your dad rather than your mum."

"Mum's not that bad," Marina protested. She was still too mad to stick up for her more strongly.

"Do you look like him?" Frankie quizzed. She knew plenty about Sinead's mother, who owned their house in Walgrave Square and visited them every so often in her designer labels and

Manolo heels. But she realized she knew zilch about Marina's folks.

"No, I'm not like either of them. Apparently I look like my gran on my dad's side when she was young. Tom takes after Mum."

"Does she go out to work?" Frankie asked.

"For a building society. She's quite high up." *And very organized, with everything totally under control. Oh and neat.* Every stitch of clothing on her back and every hair on Alice Kent's head knew exactly how to behave.

"What about your dad?" Sinead asked.

"More laid-back," Marina admitted, finishing her drink as someone came to drag her off for a facial. "Which drives Mum crazy, of course."

Sinead and Frankie watched Marina disappear down the corridor in thoughtful silence.

"What do you think?" Frankie said at last.

"Of the Kent family?" Sinead asked. "All I'd say is, I'd rather be stranded on a desert island with the water engineer than the building society lady!"

"Even though you've never met him?"

"Deffo." Sinead stood up to go and give her feet a treat in her reflexology session. "From what I can make out about Marina's mum, it's a miracle Marina's turned out anywhere near normal!"

Can u come home right away? Marina read the text from Rob.

"What time is it?" she asked Sinead, who had just turned off the hair dryer in the changing room after an additional two hours of pampering.

Frankie, always the quickest at getting ready, was out in reception, waiting for them.

"Just coming up to five o'clock." Sinead fluffed up her blond halo by turning her head upside down and shaking it. Then she sprayed it into place.

"So what does Rob want?" Marina wondered. He'd left the message for her during the massage session.

"He's probably still outside, working on his engine. He needs you to supply him with tea and biscuits."

"Maybe."

"Tell him to get his own."

Marina noticed that Rob hadn't finished off with a row of lovey-dovey *X*s—unusual for him. "I'll call him," she decided.

"Hi, Rob, it's me."

"Hi. Did you get my message?"

"Yeah, that's what I'm calling about. Why do you need me?"

Packing away her hairbrush and makeup, Sinead gestured to Marina that she'd meet her outside, then left.

"I don't *need* you." Rob hesitated then rushed on. "Listen, just come, will you?"

"Do I get the feeling that it's important?" Marina was looking into a mirror and frowning. It was unheard of for laid-back Rob to be dishing out the orders like this.

He ignored her question. "How long will you be?"

"Twenty minutes if I walk. Five if a bus comes along."

"Okay. Try to catch a bus." Rob was about to hang up when he added a final instruction. "Oh, and call at my place before you go to yours."

"What is it? Did Tim Yorke turn you down?" Marina hadn't been lucky with the buses and had run all the way to Walgrave Square. Frankie and Sinead had lagged behind.

"No, this isn't about my interview," Rob told her. "You're out of breath. Sit down. Have a drink."

She took the bottle of water that he handed her from the fridge. "What is it, then?"

"It's your father."

Marina felt a jolt run through her body. "Dad?" she asked faintly. "What's happened?" *They didn't find him after all. Or else, they did find him, but he's not okay. He's got a bad injury. He's in the hospital. Maybe he's even dead!*

"Nothing. He's fine. I asked if he wanted to wait here for you but he said he'd rather wait in the car."

"The car?"

"Yes. He's here. He showed up in the Square about an hour ago."

"My dad's here in Walgrave Square?" Reacting instinctively, Marina jumped up and headed for the door.

"I was outside working on the bike. I saw a guy knocking on your door."

"And you went over to ask him what he wanted?"

Rob nodded. "I told him who I was and he said he was your dad."

"Oh my God!" Marina cried, still intent on dashing to Number 13.

"Wait. Do you want me to come with you?"

"Where is he? Oh, that's his car outside our house! No, stay here, Rob."

"You sure?" This was a big moment for Marina. Rob didn't want to get in the way. But he felt she might need him.

Marina paused and nodded. "Oh my God, Rob—Dad's back! I can't believe it. Wait here. I have to go and see him!"

Nine

"Hey, kid, you look fantastic!" Martin Kent held Marina at arm's length to admire every inch of his glamorous, grown-up daughter. "More beautiful than ever."

"Never mind me. How are you?" She couldn't believe her eyes, even though she'd dragged her father out of his car into the house, sat him down in the front room, and hugged him a dozen times.

"I'm fine. Look at me—not a scratch!"

"So what happened?" Eager to hear the details, Marina kept hold of his hand. Her dad was back. He was sitting next to her dressed in a dark blue polo shirt and jeans, looking tired but otherwise okay.

"How much do you know?"

"Nothing! They posted you as missing. No reasons, no information."

Martin squeezed her hand. "Poor baby. It wasn't half as bad as it might have been. All that happened was that our jeep broke down—dirt in the cylinder head. Kaput. We were in the middle of nowhere, with no signal on our phones and the radio transmitter was down so we couldn't use the two-way system either."

"But you had food and water?" She tried to imagine breaking down in those circumstances—no twenty-four-hour rescue service, no nice AAA man driving up to help! "Was it hot? Were you scared?"

"There were a few hairy moments," her dad admitted. "We knew not to leave the vehicle and strike out on our own. What we did was sit tight in the jeep until a group of men from the nearest village came across us and took us back with them. They hadn't a clue who we were, but they gave us a place to sleep while a couple went off on foot to the nearest medical center, which was about seventy miles away. They showed the staff where to find us."

"Why the medical center?"

"Well, we had no common language, but Kim showed them her Médecins Sans Frontières identity card, which they recognized. They must have linked us with the aid workers at the hospital, and off they went."

Marina nodded. "Mum said all along that you'd be okay."

Martin smiled. "And she was right."

"As usual. Dad, I had to look up Niger on the atlas! I didn't even know where it was. I was really scared!"

"Poor baby," he said again. He stood up and looked out the window, across the Square to the motorbike standing outside Number 45. "I met Rob," he said quietly.

"Yeah, you missed him at Christmas." A previous foreign trip had meant that her dad hadn't met The Boyfriend at the ritual family grilling.

"He seems like a nice guy."

"He is."

Her dad turned toward her. "Does he know how lucky he is to have landed my girl?"

Marina blushed. "I'm not a fish, Dad!"

"You are—you're a catch!" he insisted with a grin.

"It's not like that anymore. If anything, *I* caught *him*!" *I dressed to kill, I hooked him, and I reeled him in!*

"But he looks after you?"

She nodded. "Rob's cool. He's a talented DJ. He could get a slot on local radio if he's lucky."

"That's great." Martin turned his back again and began to pace the room, hands in pockets.

Marina prattled on proudly. "He went for an interview yesterday. They liked him. He's waiting to hear if he got the job."

"That's a nice bike he's got."

She stopped short. "Dad, are you listening?" *There's more!* she thought. *There's something he hasn't told me yet!*

"Hmm? Yeah, he's a DJ."

"Only part-time at the moment. But he ditched his college job in order to concentrate on the deejaying. And he manages an indie band called Bad Mouth." Gradually Marina wound down until she was almost at a standstill. Her dad definitely wasn't paying attention to what she said. He stood with his head down, deep in thought. "What's wrong?" she asked quietly.

Martin looked up. "Have you seen your mother?"

"Yesterday. We drove across. Tom was there too. Why?"

"How was she?"

"In a majorly bad mood with me for some reason. I guess it's the stress."

Her dad nodded, half looked away, then took a step toward her. "She didn't say anything?"

Jeez, what is this? Oh, okay, I know what's coming, and I don't want to hear! She replied hesitantly: "No, she was pissed off with me for showing up without warning, that's all. Are you telling me you haven't you been home yet?"

"No. I needed to see you first. Then I plan to talk to Tom."

So, tell me! Come on, Dad, spit it out! Mentally Marina did a U-turn. She was ready to face whatever he was about to dump on her. "It's okay," she assured him. "I can guess what this is all about."

"All right—your mother and I have been having problems," Martin confessed. "It's been brewing up a long time, and now it's come to a head."

"You're leaving her," she said flatly. The banal words sounded odd in her mouth, as if they couldn't possibly relate to her own mum and dad.

He nodded, sighed, shook his head. He couldn't look her in the eye. "I'm sorry, Marina. I really am."

*

"I like this track," Travis told Rob.

They were in their living room, listening to music, trying to pick out chords, which Rob then tried to strum on his guitar. Across the Square, Marina was being reunited with her dad.

"Man, this is harder than it sounds." In his teens Rob had played guitar a lot, but these days he didn't practice enough. He stretched his fingers across the strings, hit a wrong note, and gave up.

"Hey, how was the interview?" Travis had turned up the volume and had to shout over the music.

"Good."

"Did you get the job?"

"Don't know yet. I hear some time next week. D'you want a coffee?"

"No, I'll have a beer."

Rob went to the fridge and fetched two cans. "Marina's dad showed up."

"He did?" Assuming this was good news, Travis grabbed the TV remote and switched on Sky Sport without volume.

"Something's not right," Rob muttered, tugging at the ring pull on his can.

"Yeah?" Travis switched off the music and turned up the volume on Arsenal versus Newcastle.

"Yeah, mate, from what I've seen, there's a definite problem out there in Upper Snobbingham!"

"Upper what? Oh yeah. You mean a problem between Marina's

mum and dad?" Newcastle had just scored. The fans went wild. "Good goal," Travis commented.

"They're on the rocks," Rob predicted, laying down his guitar and heading for the door. Marina needed him, and she needed him right now. "If anybody wants me I'm at Number 13!"

The world looked different from the backseat of a motorbike.

Marina held tight. She felt the force of the wind as Rob picked up speed, crouched lower, and stared at the road ahead.

They were on a wide A-road. It was early Sunday morning, and there was no traffic around.

Rob lifted his gloved hand from the handlebar, reached back, and touched her leg. She squeezed his waist.

Are you okay?

I'm cool.

Marina loved the speed—the way the trees lining the road became a green blur, how you had to lean into a bend, but not too much, the rush of the air against your visor.

They headed out of town, up hills and swooping down into valleys, breaking the silence with the deep roar of the engine.

"I need to clear my head," she'd told Rob as they lay in bed. Her dad had broken the bad news the night before. Rob had shown up and helped her through it. He'd mopped up her tears and together they'd waved her dad good-bye.

But she hadn't slept for thinking about her parents. If they separated, what would happen? Who would have the house?

Where would the other one live? Which one would Tom choose to be with—their mum or their dad?

Rob had gotten up and brought her tea in bed. "Let's go for a ride," he'd suggested.

And here they were.

White blossom in the hedges, blue sky overhead—the best of early English summer. The bike cut through the countryside until Rob shifted the gears to slow and then stop the bike beside a river. He steadied the bike, waiting for Marina to hop off.

They parked and walked, carrying their helmets, following the riverbank.

"How do you feel now?" he asked.

"Better."

"Not your problem, remember." He'd told her last night that it was Martin and Alice's war zone. The best Marina could do was stay away until the dust settled. "You two kids don't want to be part of the collateral damage," he'd insisted. "Y'know—where innocent civilians get zapped!"

She'd seen the sense of his argument, but she couldn't switch off from the problem as easily as that. Even now, walking by the calm, shining water, she couldn't free her mind of the scene at home—the two of them sitting down face-to-face to talk things through, her dad shamefaced, her mum boiling over with anger. "What about Tom?" she said quietly.

"He'll know the score by now."

"I wonder how he's taking it."

Rob shrugged. "The sooner he gets back to school the better. He'll be with his mates. It'll take his mind off things."

Marina stopped to stare at the water. It glided by so gently. "This sucks," she sighed, her eyes filling with tears again.

He held her tight. "It's an old, old story," he whispered. "It happened to my folks five years ago. People fall out of love. They break up."

"I never expected it to happen to us!"

Right now, when life was opening up for her, when so much was happening and she wanted to snatch every opportunity, to be good at everything and succeed in fashion design.

Right now, after her dad had disappeared and been in danger and she'd had nightmares about him staying lost forever. And after he'd shown up and everything should be happy, happy!

"My family is falling apart," she sobbed.

"But I'm here," Rob reminded her.

Marina put her arms around his neck. The river ran by their feet. They didn't have to say anything—they felt so close.

Cromer was the middle of bloody nowhere! The beach was pebbly and hurt your feet. Pebbles everywhere. Round here they even built houses out of pebbles!

At least the sun is shining, Frankie thought.

Okay, so she'd stepped off the bus and fifty years back in time, into striped sticks of rock, deckchairs, and candyfloss, but it was warm for the shoot.

"Everything has to look faded," the stylist explained. "Faded beach huts, bleached colors, white pebbles."

Bloody pebbles! Frankie stubbed her toe against one. They'd put her into a multicolored print bikini with a mini sarong, stuck a vintage straw hat in her hand, and told her to strike a pose.

"Sit on the prow of that rowing boat, love," the photographer instructed.

Frankie looked vague and had to be told which end was the prow.

"Crook one leg, lean back, look this way."

"Sunglasses!" the stylist remembered.

Frankie put them on and restruck the pose.

"More playful," the photographer insisted. "Keep it natural, tilt your head back, look this way!"

An audience of two little kids and a grandma had gathered. They watched events with a bored, nothing-else-to-do air.

Phoebe, the stylist, brought Frankie down from the yellow and white painted boat and changed her into a Luella tie-side bikini—"Very fifties!"

"Ice cream!" the littlest kid demanded, and the audience melted away, leaving only a stray dog.

"I wish I was still in Paris!" Frankie sighed, staggering over the stony beach in Viktor and Rolf red glitter shoes.

"Get rid of the dog," the photographer told Phoebe, who fluttered a piece of paper at it and said, "Shoo!"

The mutt ignored Phoebe, sniffed at Frankie's red shoes, then it too lost interest and wandered off. Who cared about La Perla Mare swimwear and Louis Vuitton suede sandals when there were waves to bark at and seagulls to chase?

"Stare out to sea," the photographer instructed after Frankie's third change of outfit. "Come on, love, give me wistful waif!"

She stared and made her mind go blank. That always worked for the wistful look.

"Watch out for the Louis Vuittons!" Phoebe shrieked, as a rogue wave came surging high up over the side.

"Honestly, I thought she was going to have a heart attack!" Frankie told Sinead. She was back home, safely surrounded by streets and shops, her feet firmly back on the flat pavement. No pebbles. "Apparently those shoes are worth 350 quid!"

"I know who will have a heart attack if we don't get these pictures on her desk first thing tomorrow," Sinead said. She'd had a cool day coloring her hair and giving herself a facial—following up the good work of yesterday. But now Frankie was back and they needed to sort out the photos.

"Yeah, I know, Claudia's on our case." Though she was tired, Frankie agreed that they had to choose which ones to mount and put into the show. "How's Marina?" she asked, kicking off her shoes and sitting cross-legged on Sinead's bedroom floor.

Frankie and Sinead had shown up the night before, soon after Martin Kent had dropped the bombshell about him and Marina's mother. Rob was already there, trying to hold Marina together.

Poor Martin hadn't known what to do or where to put himself. Eventually he'd left them to it.

"I didn't think she'd take it this badly," he'd told Sinead. "I thought that now she's left home it wouldn't hit her so hard."

But it had, and Sinead would have been able to tell him it would because she'd been there herself, and it was lucky Rob was around, because when your parents did this to you, you needed someone.

"She's okay," Sinead reported now. "Rob's looking after her. I think they decided to go out for a ride on the bike and then a Thai meal, but she said she'd be back later. She wants to get some college stuff ready for tomorrow."

Frankie glanced at her watch. "I need to be in bed by midnight. That gives us an hour and a half to do this."

Sinead spread the photographs across the floor. It felt weird to be studying so many images of herself. "You're going to be better at this than me," she told Frankie. "It's hard for me to cut off and be objective."

"Well, this is a good shot, and this, and this." Quickly Frankie picked out the ones that worked best in terms of lighting and angles. "Travis did a great job. Does he say he can crop and edit these for us, once we've made a decision?"

"Not by tomorrow. But by Wednesday he can."

"That'll give us a day and a half to mount and hang them for the show."

Putting their heads together, concentrating, Sinead and

Frankie got through a lot of work, until a ring on the doorbell interrupted them.

"Huh!" Frankie looked again at her watch and saw that it was a quarter to midnight.

"Maybe Marina forgot her key." Sinead was closer to the door, so she went downstairs.

The bell rang again.

"Okay, okay where's the fire?" Sinead called, fiddling with the lock before she could open the door.

A woman stood there. She was tall, about thirty years old, with long, straight brown hair and a serious face. "I'm sorry to bother you," she said.

Sinead kept the door half closed, a barrier between her and the stranger. "I was expecting someone else."

"Yes, I know it's late." The woman's expression and soft voice seemed to convey an appeal to Sinead not to shut the door in her face. "I'm looking for someone. I think he might be here."

Sinead shook her head, assuming there must be a mistake. "I don't think so."

"This is Number 13?"

"Who is it?" Frankie called, running downstairs.

"Yes, this is Number 13," Sinead said, gesturing for Frankie to hang back and let her deal with it.

Frankie ignored the warning and joined her at the door. "What's up?" she demanded. "We don't know you, do we?"

"No." The caller hitched up the collar of her denim jacket. She faltered her way through the next sentence. "The guy I'm looking for—his name's Martin Kent."

Sinead frowned. Frankie stared hard at the woman. What was the connection between her and Marina's dad, they wondered.

They came to the answer together.

"God, no!" Frankie groaned.

"You're the Médecins Sans Frontières woman!" Sinead gasped.

It dawned on them—the reason Marina's dad had left her mum was standing right there on the doorstep!

"That's right—I'm Kim Cosgrove," she told them. "I was wondering—is Martin here?"

Ten

"We have to get rid of her!" Frankie decided.

She and Sinead had stuck Kim in the front room then retreated to the kitchen.

"How can we?" Sinead demanded. She'd felt sorry for the woman and let her into the house. "It's nearly midnight. She's got nowhere to go!"

"She's not staying here!"

Sinead sighed then nodded.

"We've got to turf her out before Marina gets back. Think about it—the last person she wants to bump into at this moment in time is her dad's mistress!"

"We don't know that's what she is." Sinead refused to jump to conclusions. All Kim Cosgrove had said was that she wanted to speak to Martin Kent. She hadn't given a reason.

"Jeez!" Frankie hissed. "Don't be so naive! Why else would the woman be chasing him halfway across the world?"

"A million reasons." Sinead closed her eyes to give herself

thinking space. Okay, so this was definitely the woman who had been listed missing along with Marina's dad. They had probably been flown back from Niger together and she'd ended up stranded in a city where she didn't know anyone and hadn't been able to find, or couldn't afford, a hotel. In that case, it was only natural that she'd be trying to link up with Martin again. Not that they could help there—Marina hadn't told them where Martin had gone.

"You're only defending her because she's Irish," Frankie pointed out. "Either that, or you live on a different planet from the rest of us!"

"Shh, keep your voice down!" Sinead knew they couldn't stay huddled in the kitchen for much longer. She'd promised the visitor a mug of tea and got busy with the kettle and a tea bag.

Frankie perched on the edge of the table, drumming her fingers on the wooden surface. "She has to drink that double quick then leave."

"Where will she go? She can't stay at Travis's house, because Rob's there and he'll figure it out and tell Marina."

Automatically Frankie racked her brains. "Hey, what am I doing? Why am I even trying to help?"

"Because . . ." Because she looked vulnerable, standing on their doorstep. Because she'd been through a bad ordeal in Niger. Because they had no idea what was really going on.

Slowly Frankie nodded. Sinead was too soft, as usual, but on the other hand, she did have a point about not throwing the poor woman out onto the street. "I'll ring Lee," she decided. "I know he has a spare room at his place."

Leaving Frankie to make the call, Sinead took the drink to their unexpected guest. "Sorry it took so long," she apologized.

Kim stood by the window. "I shouldn't have come. I've made things awkward for you."

"It's cool," Sinead insisted. "You've had a long journey. You must be tired."

"This must seem strange." Attempting an uneasy smile, Kim started to offer an explanation. "I knew Martin was planning to see his daughter. I wanted to speak to him first."

"You missed him. He came here yesterday." Sinead looked closely at the Médecins Sans Frontières worker, trying to figure her out. She looked lean and fit, like a female TV journalist reporting from a war zone in the Middle East, dressed in light, loose trousers, the denim jacket, and a white T-shirt. Her face was a good shape—rather square, with straight eyebrows and a high forehead. "How did you know where Marina lives?" she asked.

"Martin told me in passing. He mentioned the Square. He talks about his daughter a lot."

And you have a good memory! Sinead thought. "Like I said, you've missed him. But if you're looking for somewhere to stay . . ."

"No, really. I'm fine!"

". . . Frankie is phoning a guy we know who lives nearby. He has a spare room where you could sleep, at least for tonight."

*

"Hi, Lee. It's me, Frankie."

"What time is it?"

"Midnight. Sorry, did I wake you up?" She pictured him fumbling with the phone in the dark, squinting to see his watch

"No, it's cool. Where are you?"

"I'm at home. But listen, Lee—you know your spare room?" The one he'd rented out to Wim before Christmas, only Juggler Wim hadn't paid any rent and had ended up breaking his landlord's heart by going out with Frankie, before stealing his iPod and other possessions and sodding off with an ex-girlfriend who was an acrobat. But that was another story. Another broken heart.

"What about it?" Lee mumbled.

"Can someone come and sleep in it?"

"It's full of junk."

"Does it have a bed?"

"No. A mattress on the floor."

"That's cool. I'll lend her a sleeping bag. She can bring it round."

"'She'?"

Okay, so now Lee was sitting up in bed, the duvet was slipping off the side. He was standing up, and he wasn't wearing any clothes . . . *Hey, quit that!* Frankie told herself. "We'll be knocking on your door in fifteen minutes," she told him firmly. "See you. Bye!"

"I've tried to call Martin, but his phone's switched off." Hastily Kim finished her tea and picked up the small rucksack she'd been carrying when Sinead had invited her into the house. She'd refused point blank the offer of a place to stay, but on her way out, she paused to ask one last favor. "Can you tell me where he went after he left here?"

Sinead shook her head. "No, sorry." Marina hadn't told them where he'd gone. Anyway, she thought she heard a motorbike pull up outside.

"Lee says it's cool!" Frankie announced, reappearing from the back of the house. She too heard the bike. *Serious bad timing!*

"No, it's okay. I don't want to put you to any trouble," Kim insisted, picking up on the startled glances and quickly guessing the reason.

"That's Marina," Sinead gasped.

"She ought not to see you," Frankie said bluntly. "She might wonder why you're here. I know I would!"

"It's okay, I can explain things to her." At the sound of steps coming up the path, Kim nervously faced the door.

Frankie grabbed her arm. "No way!" she said, dragging the visitor down the corridor.

Kim resisted. "Let go of me!"

"Let her go," Sinead pleaded with Frankie.

"No, she can leave by the back way. We have to get her out without upsetting Marina!"

A key turned in the door.

"Yeah, do that!" Sinead urged, suddenly panicking and changing her mind. She too began to hustle Kim into the kitchen.

Marina opened the door. There were three figures scuffling in her hallway. "What the heck is happening here?" she said.

Kim Cosgrove was the first to pull it back together.

("How did she *do* that?" Frankie asked Sinead later, after the dust had settled. "You have to admire the cool nerve of the woman!")

She freed herself from Frankie and Sinead then introduced herself to Marina. "I'm a work colleague of your father's from Médecins Sans Frontières."

"Hey, and here's me thinking we had burglars," Marina said with a frown, dumping her helmet on the floor. Like with Frankie and Sinead, a split second had been enough for her to compute what was really going on here. *Médecins Sans Frontières. Mariages Sans Frontières!*

"Maybe we do," Frankie said darkly. You could steal other people's husbands, as well as their TVs and jewelry.

"I wanted to speak to him, but he has his phone switched off," Kim tried to explain, braving out the hostility but barely able to hold herself together now.

"I expect that means he doesn't want to speak to you," Marina countered. "Especially at this time of night. And especially considering he's not here."

"That's what we told her," Frankie broke in.

Marina narrowed her eyes and spoke each word with slow, heavy emphasis. "Actually, he's speaking to my mum, probably at this very moment, telling her that he wants a divorce."

Frankie and Sinead gasped.

("She totally laid it on the line!" Sinead recalled, during the postmortem with Frankie.)

Kim's eyes widened. She let her bag drop from her shoulder but caught it in time to stop it from dropping to the floor.

Marina's gaze was blazing with anger, though her voice was still steady. "That wouldn't have anything to do with you by any chance?"

"Listen!" Kim began.

Marina advanced down the hall toward her.

("Like Halle Berry in *Catwoman*, in skintight leathers, claws out!" Frankie said, full of awe.)

"No, listen, let me explain!"

"There's nothing to explain," Marina argued. "My father's divorcing my mother after he spends a couple of nights stuck in a jeep with you. It's not hard to work out."

Sinead stepped in between Kim and Marina. "Wait!" she warned.

"You could at least have the decency to let him get the confessions over with before you show up!" Marina said, her voice rising. "Or are you scared he'll change his mind? Is that why you're so keen to speak to him?"

Pressed back against the bottom step of the stairs, Kim changed tack. "I'm sorry, I shouldn't have come. It's not appropriate. I'll leave."

Marina was less than twelve inches from Kim's face, spitting out her words. "'Not appropriate'! Did you think it was *appropriate* when you started an affair with a guy twenty years older than you, who happens to be married and has two kids?"

"Hold it, Marina," Sinead pleaded. "We can't be sure—"

"Butt out, Sinead. Let me do this my way." Riding her anger now, still face-to-face with the woman who'd wrecked her home, Marina tore into Kim. "You have a nerve, showing up here. This is my place, you hear? I don't want your stinking, rotten presence anywhere near!"

"Let's go!" Frankie told Kim, dragging her sideways out of Marina's reach and squeezing her down the corridor.

She'd opened the door and felt the cold night air on her face, had hustled Kim down the path before she heard the sound of the gate squeaking on its hinges and looked up.

"Hey, Frankie," Lee said, appearing out of nowhere. "Do you still need my spare room?"

Eleven

The next morning, Frankie and Sinead took the bus into college.

"Man, I'm tired!" Sinead sighed. She could hardly keep her eyes open as the bus swayed around a corner and braked for traffic.

"Yeah, me too. I only got three hours' sleep," Frankie yawned.

"Lee was pretty cool, though."

"Hmm."

"He was!" Sinead insisted. "He's a good mate to drag himself out of bed and come and fetch Kim."

"You didn't hear him going on about being woken up at midnight," Frankie argued. "All the way back to his place he was moaning about missing his sleep and having to clear the junk out of the spare room."

"Oh, so that's why you went to Nugent Road?"

"Yeah, to help clear the room," Frankie insisted. "Why? What are you saying?"

"*Moi?*" Sinead faked innocence.

"Yeah, you! I didn't have an ulterior motive, if that's what you think."

"Not even a teeny smidgeon?"

"No!" Frankie told herself not to let Sinead get to her. She brushed the unspoken subject of Lee's fancy-ability to one side. "How about Marina eyeballing Kim the way she did?"

Sinead drew a deep breath. "We nearly had a catfight on our hands."

"I was impressed. I didn't know Marina had the guts." Gazing out of the window at the damp streets, Frankie wondered if she would have had the nerve to confront Kim as Marina had done.

"How was Kim when you got to Lee's place?"

"Quiet. She obviously didn't want to talk."

"So she didn't say anything?"

"About Marina's dad? Nope, zilch." Frankie had gathered that the woman was in a state of shock about the whole thing and had just wanted to curl up in a sleeping bag and make it go away.

Sinead shook her head in disbelief. "What was she thinking, chasing him to his daughter's place?" She pictured the emotional whirlpool of love, jealousy, and fear that Kim and Martin had been dragged into, then answered her own question. "She was desperate, I guess."

"Don't ask me. All I know is, she shouldn't have done it." Seeing their stop, Frankie stood up and squeezed past standing passengers toward the exit. "Look what she did to Marina," she added, glancing over her shoulder to check that Sinead could manage their portfolio of photographs in the crush.

They made it onto the pavement then made a dash for the shelter of the college entrance, out of the rain. Sinead used the sleeve of her jacket to wipe splashes from the plastic cover of the portfolio. "People do weird stuff under pressure," she went on. "Logic flies out of the window."

"Yeah well, don't you start feeling sorry for Kim Cosgrove." Frankie pushed through the swing doors and marched along the corridor ahead of Sinead. "She's a grown woman. She should take responsibility for what she does."

Sinead picked up speed to draw level. "She's not your usual home-wrecker type." Definitely not the plunging-neckline, streaked hair, perma-tan sort of woman.

Frankie stopped short. She was tired, and she didn't care about the details, only about Marina and the effect this was having on her. "Drop it, okay?" she told Sinead.

Sinead nodded. "Yeah, sorry." They walked on toward Claudia's office. "So, come on, Frankie, admit it," she teased, returning to her earlier tactic. "Lee tried it on and asked you to stay the night!"

"No way!"

"He did."

"Did not!" She and Lee had cleared the junk from the mattress, Kim had kipped down straight away, Lee had offered Frankie a drink, and she'd said no and gone straight home. End of story.

*

There was a note pinned to the door of Claudia's office. MONDAY, ALL DAY—WORKING IN EXHIBITION HALL 2. URGENT INTERRUPTIONS ONLY.

"Are we urgent?" Sinead asked Frankie. The fiery jewelry tutor scared the pants off her. "Couldn't we just leave the portfolio in the office?"

"No," Frankie decided. "We need Claudia's go-ahead on the pictures we've chosen."

So they went back downstairs, following the smell of fresh paint into the huge, high room where the first year students would exhibit their work. They found men up ladders, paint sheets on the floor, white partitions stacked against walls, plinths blocking their way, and, in the distance, Claudia issuing orders.

"We need two partitions at this end of the room!" she instructed. "I've put chalk lines on the floor. No, not that one. This mark here!"

Two second year students had been press-ganged to fetch and carry. Slowly they edged a partition into place.

"Let's come back later," Sinead suggested. Her confidence was ebbing away by the second.

"Get a grip," Frankie told her, though the nerves were getting to her too. What if it turned out that Claudia hated what they'd done and made them ditch the whole project? Okay, so Travis's photos were excellent, but that wasn't to say that Sinead's body art and her own jewelry would pass the test.

Across the room, the tutor disappeared behind a tall screen.

"She's busy right now," Sinead insisted, clutching the portfolio tight to her body.

Dithering in the doorway, they were on the point of running away when Tristan Fox came up from behind and bundled them into the room. "Calamity!" he exclaimed. "Major crisis! Where's Claudia? Has anybody seen Claudia?"

"Over there." A painter up a ladder nodded in the jewelry tutor's direction.

Tristan dashed on. "Claudia, do you have the floor plan for Friday? There's been an accident. Stop everything!"

As Claudia appeared from behind the screen, clipboard in hand, Frankie and Sinead stayed to listen.

"Accident?" Claudia asked, suspicious and severe.

"One of the students, Katrine . . ."

"Walker?" Sinead offered.

"Yes, Katrine Walker is in the hospital with a concussion and a broken foot. The stupid girl went rock climbing over the weekend. She fell five meters."

"That's impossible!" Claudia exclaimed. "She's supposed to be in college this morning, finishing off her exhibits. She had plenty left to do."

"Exactly." Tristan allowed Claudia to absorb the full impact of his news. "What on earth was the idiot girl thinking, climbing a cliff face on the weekend before the show!"

Frankie leaned sideways and whispered to Sinead, "No sympathy there, then!"

"Not even a smidgen," Sinead murmured.

In the middle of the room, Claudia and Tristan assessed the situation. "Should we move her exhibition slot to a more out-of-the-way corner, just in case her exhibits aren't ready?" asked Claudia.

"That's why I need the floor plan," Tristan explained, his normally suave and superior manner nowhere to be seen. This was big-time crisis for the Head of Department. "If we have to move Katrine's work from this space by the entrance, whose do we put in its place?"

"It has to be someone good," Claudia muttered. "Listen, I'm reluctant to move Katrine until we know more about her injuries and how near to finishing her work she is. A move now would throw us into complete chaos."

Reluctantly Tristan agreed. "Daisy Fenwick is planning to go and see Katrine this afternoon. Perhaps she'll have more news. But how long can we afford to wait?"

"Until tomorrow morning," Claudia insisted.

"At the very latest." Turning back toward the door, Tristan noticed Sinead and Frankie once more. He sighed and shook his head. "Rock climbing!" Then, as he rushed past them, a thought struck him. "Where's your friend, Marina?" he asked Sinead. "Is she in college?"

"Actually, no," Sinead replied warily. The last she had seen of Marina was last night, after Kim Cosgrove had been carted off to Nugent Road.

"Well, when you next see her, tell her to stand by," Tristan said in a flurry of exasperated hand gestures. "Tell her, the way things are going, there's every chance that her work will take pride of place in Friday's show!"

"Portfolio!" Claudia pointed to Sinead and Frankie's photographs and marched them upstairs to her room.

They followed like sheep to the slaughter.

"The lady is not in a good mood!" Frankie whispered.

"She's going to rip us to shreds!" Sinead predicted.

They walked along, fully expecting to be failed and kicked out of college.

Daniella will kill me! Sinead thought.

Here it comes again—the end of my dream! was Frankie's miserable view.

I've dragged Frankie down with me, Sinead concluded.

We pushed the experiment too far. We were too way-out and ambitious. Frankie prepared herself for rejection.

"Close the door," Claudia ordered. She took the portfolio from Sinead and laid it on her table. Opening it, she viewed the first photograph, slowly turned it facedown and went on to the next one.

She hates them! Frankie thought.

That's it, they're no good. Finito!

Claudia bowed her head to study each picture. She traced her forefinger along the curved lines of Frankie's arm band and over the intricate patterns of Sinead's body art.

The seconds ticked by and turned into silent minutes. Frankie noticed odd things, like the crude clay model of a man in glasses, scratching his head, sitting on the tutor's bookshelf, obviously done by a kid. She wondered who had made it. Sinead stared at the top of Claudia's head, at her tightly drawn back, dark hair and the bold pair of hooped gold earrings loaded down with tiny charms.

At last Claudia had examined all the pictures and raised her head to look at Frankie and Sinead. "Okay," she said.

Okay? Sinead stared at Frankie. Had she heard right?

Okay? Frankie's mouth dropped open.

"Okay, go ahead," Claudia insisted. She zipped up the folder and pushed it toward them. "Get these mounted and ready for showing."

"You like them?" Sinead checked.

She likes them! Frankie echoed inside her head.

Claudia raised her eyebrows a fraction. "They won't be to everybody's taste," she pointed out. "But I find them innovative and extremely interesting."

Wow! Sinead grabbed the portfolio.

"Thanks!" Frankie gasped, escaping from the room. *Lordy, Lordy, thank you!*

It was Marina's decision to go home on the train, no one else's.

"Are you sure you want to do this?" Rob had asked, walking her to the station. "You know what happened last time."

"I'm sure," she'd insisted. "Dad will still be there. And Tom, I expect. I need to find out what's going on." *Exactly why my family is falling apart.*

"Text me when you get there," he'd made her promise.

And he'd stood at the end of the platform, waving as she got onto the train, waiting until it had drawn out of the station.

Marina sat opposite a business type in shirtsleeves, his ear glued to his mobile phone.

"Shirley, line up a meeting with Will Sutton for tomorrow afternoon, please . . . Yes, Gary, good news—we're up two whole percentage points . . . Hi, honey. I'm on the train . . ."

Blocking out his voice and trying to avoid his big feet under the table, Marina stared out the window, only to find that her own reflection got in the way of the green fields and horses grazing. *What-a-mess, what-a-mess!* the rhythm of the train on the track seemed to say.

She opened a book and tried to read. *I should be in college finishing my project*, she told herself. *Mum's going to go mad when I turn up on the doorstep.*

Rob sent her a text and she read it. Love u xxxxxxx

Love u 2 xxxxxxxxxxxx, she texted back.

"No, I won't be late," Phone-bloke promised. "I have one meeting at two-thirty. That means I should be home by seven. Love you, bye."

Why did the journey seem so long? Marina wondered. Why did Phone-bloke's nose hair fascinate and repel her? Why couldn't he keep his feet to himself?

"Tea? Coffee?" The trolley girl came by.

Phone-bloke bought coffee and a Kit-Kat.

What-a-mess, what-a-mess, what-a-mess.

Marina looked ahead a couple of hours. She would arrive at the house and there would be no cars in the cul-de-sac except her mum and dad's. Everyone else would be at work. The cherry blossom tree in the front garden would be in full bloom. She would use her own key.

Her mum would be stone-faced. Tom would be in his room watching TV. Her dad would probably be packing.

What-a-mess.

And all for a do-gooder called Kim who worked for practically nothing for a medical setup in third-world countries. Who was nearer Marina's age than her dad's.

Marina frowned deeply then closed her eyes. What age was Kim? she wondered. Thirty, maybe. If that.

She pictured again the moment when she'd first set eyes on the woman who was wrecking their lives. Kim had struggled free of Frankie and Sinead then stood up straight to face Marina in the hallway.

Of course! Marina had thought in a flash. *This is the other woman!* Suddenly everything had slotted into place—her dad's guilt over leaving her mum, her mum's lack of relief when her dad had been found, which meant that her mum had already suspected the affair and was driven by jealousy when the two had vanished together in darkest Africa.

Poor Mum! Marina had thought.

And straight away she'd assessed the rival—tallish, fairly attractive, but not stunning. She looked tough and capable on the outside, like someone who would take charge in a crisis, and yet, standing in Marina's house, like someone who was vulnerable on the inside, whom she would have felt sorry for if the situation had been different.

Don't weaken! Marina told herself as the train rattled on. *Don't even consider that woman's feelings!*

She was on her way home to talk to her dad before he made the biggest mistake of his life. She would take her mother's side and fight for the family.

Her mother! Marina pictured her side by side with Kim Cosgrove. One neat, controlled, precise, and middle-aged. The other all-action, intense, clever, and young.

Young. Yes, that was what this was all about.

Marina texted Rob, Arrived safe xxxx, and turned off her phone. This was her station, her family mess that she was walking into the middle of.

Twelve

Frankie couldn't believe her eyes.

Lee had just shown up in the college coffee bar with Kim Cosgrove.

"What are you doing?" she demanded, standing up and almost knocking over her chair.

Lee shrugged. "I couldn't stop her. She wouldn't leave without talking to you."

Frankie turned on Kim. One free night on Lee's mattress was enough, surely, without coming in here and pushing her luck. "What is this? What have you got to say that could possibly make any difference to the fact that you've barged in and wrecked four people's lives?"

Kim flinched under the attack. "It wasn't like that."

"No? Are you saying you didn't know Martin Kent was married?"

Kim shook her head.

"At least you're not denying the affair." Aware that other people in the coffee bar might be listening, Frankie went outside into the corridor with Kim and Lee. "So why was it so mega important for you to see him last night? Hadn't you had all the time you needed, out in Niger?"

"It's not like that," Kim said again. "Neither of us wanted this to happen."

Frankie gave an ironic click of her fingers. "So it was magic, just like that!"

"No. Yes. We fell in love. Not just this last week. I first met Martin two years ago."

"Perfect!" Frankie groaned. "He's been cheating on his wife for two whole years!"

"Listen!" Kim pleaded. "We fell in love without meaning to. Both of us have tried to end it in the past, but something—maybe fate—kept throwing us back together. Okay, I know how that sounds."

"It sounds phony," Frankie said bluntly. "Like you're trying to wriggle out of taking the blame."

"Maybe." It was obviously painful for Kim to go on, but she pushed herself. "Last week in Niger, it was very difficult. We were in danger when the jeep broke down. Martin said, if we got out of it, then he would go straight home and tell Alice the marriage was over. That finally he wanted to be with me."

"And?" Frankie prompted.

"I thought it was what I wanted too."

"But?"

"But on the flight back, in the airport when we said good-bye, and afterward when I knew he was telling the whole family about the decision, I was thinking and feeling a thousand different things, that maybe in the end it wasn't the right course of action . . ."

"Let me get this clear," Frankie interrupted. "Why *did* you come to Walgrave Square last night?"

"To find Martin. Like I said, he'd switched off his phone."

"To tell him what?" an exasperated Frankie asked, spreading her hands and rolling her eyes at Lee.

"That I wanted him to back off for a while," Kim explained. "So not to tell Alice that he wanted a divorce, because I wasn't able to give him the commitment he was looking for, not right now."

"You're dumping him?" Frankie cried. "And now you want me to tell Marina so she can pass the message on to her dad before the whole thing goes up in smoke!"

"Flaming Nora!" Travis said when Frankie told him. Sinead added words that a good Catholic girl shouldn't know.

Frankie had tracked them both down in the photography technician's room and made her announcement. "I know, it's a total mess!" she agreed.

"Where is this chick—what's her name?" Travis asked.

"Kim Cosgrove. She just left here with Lee. I told him to get her to the station and put her on a train—anywhere, so long as she's not still hanging around here for Marina to bump into."

"Where's Marina?" Sinead asked. "Did she go to Rob's?"

Travis rubbed the stubble on his chin. "Let's think. Yeah, she was there this morning, but she left before I did."

"Well, she didn't come back to Number 13." Frankie frowned. "Did Rob say where she was going? Come on, Travis, think!"

When the answer finally came to him, through a blur of half-awake, early morning autopilot and the haze of a hangover, the news wasn't good. "She's gone to see her parents," he recalled.

Sinead groaned.

"Oh nightmare!" Frankie sighed. She was beginning to feel claustrophobic. "More coffee!" she pleaded.

So they headed out of the cupboard-size room in search of the nearest vending machine. They hit a huddle of first years outside Tristan's room and heard the name "Katrine Walker" being noisily discussed.

". . . She broke her ankle!"

". . . Daisy said she went unconscious."

". . . Immobilized . . . in plaster . . . physiotherapy . . ."

"The whole world is falling apart!" Sinead murmured.

"Frankie, come and see me first thing tomorrow. Bring your jewelry for the show." Claudia dashed by, her hands and face streaked with white paint, her hair escaping and falling untidily around her shoulders. "And Sinead, I need to see your original designs—all the preparation work. It has to go into the show so that we can see the full creative process."

"Excuse me while my head messily explodes!" Frankie groaned.

"Coffee!" Travis took charge and led the way. They found a

machine and he put coins in the slot. Then they went outside and sat by the fountain at the main entrance.

For a while no one said anything.

Sinead stared deep into her paper cup, swishing the hot black liquid to and fro without lifting it to her lips.

Frankie was remembering how Marina had looked in that split second the night before, when she'd slotted Kim Cosgrove into the picture. Totally shocked. Angry. Hurt.

"I should never have let that woman in the house," Sinead said at last. "Frankie told me to get rid of her," she explained to Travis, who put his arm around her shoulder.

"Yeah well, there's no point shutting the stable door after the milk has been spilled, or whatever." Frankie managed a grin.

"Excuse her mixed metaphor," Travis added.

"No, I mean, it happened and that's that. Anyhow, Kim Cosgrove is trouble waiting to happen. If she hadn't come looking for Martin Kent at our house, she would've gone straight to their place in the country. It would've kicked off there instead."

"But does he know she's dumping him?" Travis asked.

Sinead glanced at Frankie, who struck her forehead with the flat of her hand and said, "Doh!"

"I know, I'm only a bloke," he shrugged. "I take it he doesn't know."

"More to the point, neither does Marina," Sinead pointed out. "Y'know, I really hate the way she's been dragged into the middle of this. She doesn't deserve it."

"Who does?" Frankie added. "But I'm with you there. Marina's a totally cool person. She has her head screwed on. She knows exactly what she wants."

"Yeah, and there's never any trampling over other people to get it." Come to think of it, Sinead had never heard Marina say a mean word about anyone. "Remember those blogs she used to write?"

"Yeah, 'Hello, world!' Totally up front and funny."

There was another silence. Behind them, the fountain shot water into the air and the wind blew shiny droplets onto their heads.

"We've got to do something," Sinead said.

"Text her," Travis suggested.

Sinead took out her phone.

"Better call her and talk to her direct," Frankie decided. "Tell her that Saint Kim is doing a runner!"

Marina felt like the condemned man taking his last walk to the electric chair. She'd opened this gate and trodden this path to her house a million times, but never with this sense of a world coming to an end.

Her mother opened the door before she had a chance to turn her key in the lock. "Come in," Alice said quietly.

Well, that's a surprise—no frown, no disapproving look, no "What are you doing here?"

"Where's Dad?" Marina asked, walking into the lounge.

"He went out for a walk. He said he needed to clear his head."

"Tom?"

"Up in his room. Marina, Dad has told me he's leaving."

"I know." The words fell flat. They still didn't seem to have any emotion attached to them. "He called to see me before he came here."

"It didn't come out of the blue. I've been living on a knife-edge for years."

Marina stared out the window at the mower that had been abandoned in the middle of the lawn. "How do you feel?" she asked.

"Numb. Now that it's come to it, I just feel empty. I'm worried about Tom."

"Tom will be okay." Oughtn't there to be hugs and tears, pleas and recriminations? The house was eerily quiet.

"Dad says there's no one else involved," Alice went on.

Marina's eyes widened. She said nothing.

"I don't necessarily believe him, mind you. It stands to reason—no man walks out on his wife and family without lining up another option—a younger model, a secretary at the office, a girl he met in a bar."

The face of Kim Cosgrove—her dark, definite features, her high forehead and serious mouth—pushed itself to the front of Marina's mind.

"Martha Hill next door was telling me a ludicrous story about her brother-in-law." Uncharacteristically, Marina's mother seemed not to want to stop talking. "The man is forty-five years old and he's just left his wife and kids for a cage-dancer. Did you even know there was such a thing? It's like a pole-dancer, apparently, only they perform inside a cage! Isn't that supremely ridiculous?"

"Mum!" Marina whispered.

There were tears in Alice's eyes as she approached Marina and took her hand. "Would you go up and see Tom?" she begged. "Since this all blew up he hasn't said a word!"

"Rob might be getting a job in local radio," Marina told her brother, to break the ice. At home, during school holidays, Tom did some deejaying at friends' parties. "And his band, Bad Mouth, might be getting a record deal."

"Huh."

"Don't sound so impressed!"

Tom sat at his computer with his back turned. He clicked his mouse and scrolled down the screen.

Marina sat on the bed. "Mum sent me to talk to you."

"What's to talk about?" Tom's voice was raw and muffled, dead set on giving nothing away.

"I know, it sucks." She looked at the posters of motorbikes and racing cars lining the walls. She sat a long time, then sighed and said, "Never mind, Tom, only three more years before you leave home to go to university!"

Martin Kent's walk turned into a three-hour hike and Marina had helped her mother finish mowing the lawn and had time to check in with Rob before he showed any sign of returning.

"How are things?" Rob asked. He was in Escape, waiting for Sinead and Travis to show up.

"Miserable. Mum's pretty calm though. Tom's gone totally into his shell."

"Babe, do you want me to ride out and fetch you?"

Like a knight on a red Yamaha, saving the maiden from the dragon of family meltdown! "No thanks," she sighed. "I didn't say anything to Mum about this Kim woman, but I want Dad to know that I know. As soon as I've spoken to him I'll catch the train back."

"Sure?"

"Yes," she insisted. "Listen, babe, I've just spotted a text from Sinead. I want to read it."

"Okay, speak to you later."

"Yes, love you, bye!" Marina opened the text from Sinead.

Hi, Marina. It's me. This important. F, T, and I learned something. Jeez, wish u didn't turn ur phone off! Anyhow, this is it. K Cosgrove has fessed up to F. Now not sure she wants to run away with ur dad & play happy ever after. In fact right this min is sprinting in opposite direction! Ur dad high & dry. I mean it—K changed mind—wanted to fess last night. Ring when u get this message. Thinking of u. xxx

Hold on! Kim Cosgrove is ditching Dad! Marina paced up and down the lawn. *Dad is leaving Mum and he doesn't have anywhere to go!*

"Marina!" Alice Kent appeared at the back door and pointed up the hill, warning her that Martin was in sight. "Come in and let him take his boots off and settle down before you talk to him."

But Marina shook her head and set off quickly up the garden, through the small gate leading onto the field. She began to run to meet her father.

"You lied!" Marina hit out with the side of her fist at Martin's chest. "You lied about Kim Cosgrove!"

His face was white, his lips thin and stretched. "I didn't lie," he protested, standing firm but turning his head to one side.

"Yes, you didn't tell me about her! That's the same as lying!"

Two ponies in the field trotted into a far corner. Her dad leaned back against the stone wall.

"And you told Mum there was no one else!"

"I didn't want to hurt her."

"Liar!"

"I wanted to make it as easy as I could."

"For you. Not for her!" Tears streamed down Marina's face. "I've seen the woman, did you know?"

Martin shook his head. He buried his face in his hands.

"That's what happens when you switch off your phone. She comes running to my house to find you!"

He groaned.

"That's right—I saw Little Miss Goody Two Shoes in the flesh. I was gobsmacked. She didn't look your type!"

"Will you stop this, Marina!"

"For a start, you're old enough to be her father!"

"I said, stop!"

Marina caught her breath. She was shaking all over, beginning to back away. She didn't see her father—the big, strong man who had play-fought on the living-room carpet when she was three years old and given her shoulder-carries. The man she'd always looked up to. Instead she saw the face of a betrayer. "There's a twenty-year age gap. What makes you think she'd stay with you?" she asked, getting ready to twist the knife.

"Okay, that's enough." He spoke more calmly now, father to daughter, defending himself.

She's leaving you! Marina wanted to say. But the words wouldn't come.

Martin spoke instead. "I know you're upset. I understand. And I'm sorry. I am, truly sorry!"

"Tell Mum that," she whispered. "That you're sorry you're putting her through hell."

"I know." He hung his head. "Listen, she and I have talked until we're sick of talking. We've gone over and over the things that went wrong."

Except for the minor detail of a mistress! Marina thought.

"And I've decided to pack up the things I need as quickly as I can and then leave. Your mother agrees it's for the best."

Again Marina felt the urge to pummel his chest. "If I were you I'd call Kim's number first," she told him, feeling that, whatever happened, he had the right to know the full truth. "I've heard she has something important to tell you."

Thirteen

"Here, Marina, get this down you." Frankie forced a slice of toast and marmalade into her hand.

Marina shook her head.

"Come on! It's Sinead who stops eating when she's under stress, not you!"

"Sorry, I can't." She'd been up all night, wandering about the house, her mind flicking from one tearful scene to the next in a crazy, confused action-replay.

"She won't eat," Frankie reported to Sinead, who had finally put in an appearance. Frankie had already been looking after Marina and listening to her run through yesterday's events for at least an hour.

Sinead glanced at her watch. "We have to see Claudia," she reminded Frankie. But one look at Marina's pale, traumatized face told her they weren't going anywhere. "Oh babe," she said, sitting down opposite her at the kitchen table. "Was it really that bad?"

"Worse," Frankie reported, sitting next to Marina and putting her arm around her shoulder. "Marina got dragged right into the middle of it. She couldn't bring herself to tell her dad about Kim the Amazing Vanishing Woman, and why should she? It's not her mess!"

"I told him to call her," Marina murmured. "Then I left."

Sinead sighed. "Yeah, I don't blame you."

"I couldn't stick around. I yelled at him and told him to ring her. God knows what happened next. I don't even know what difference it would make if Kim dumps him—he's still left Mum!"

"Cool," Sinead insisted. "That's so what I would have done!"

"Why couldn't I hack it?" Marina turned her miserable face into Frankie's shoulder and sobbed. "I lost it with him. I was yelling and yelling."

"He let you down," Frankie soothed. "He's your father. That's not the way it's supposed to be."

Sinead let her cry for a while. "What about Rob? How did he handle it?"

"Totally amazing," Marina told her. "He met me off the train. I didn't have to say anything—he took one look at me and understood."

"Let's face it, he wouldn't have to be a mind reader," Frankie pointed out. "I mean, to be honest, we've seen you look better!"

Marina managed a faint smile, so Frankie ran with it. "She gets off the train looking tragic—no makeup, hair is a bird's nest, linen trousers creased to hell—she falls into Rob's arms and blubs like a baby!"

"Don't exaggerate," Marina protested.

"I'm not. Rob takes one look at the blotchy face, the bags under the eyes, the snotty nose . . ."

"Puh-lease!" Sinead was relieved that Frankie had lightened the mood. "I really rate Rob," she decided.

"Yeah, he's definitely a for-better-or-for-worse guy."

"For richer, for poorer."

"In sickness and in health," Frankie concluded. "Hey, did he hear about his job interview yet?"

Marina shook her head. "He says he thinks he didn't get it."

"You're sure you don't want this toast?" Standing up, Frankie began to clear the breakfast debris from the table, then, when the phone rang, she went to answer it.

"Hello," she said, reaching over the back of the sofa in the front room and fishing out the phone from under the cushions.

"Hi—Frankie?"

"Yeah, who's this?"

"It's Lee."

"Oh, hi, Lee." Not someone she was expecting. As usual, Frankie's defenses went up.

"I thought I'd fill you in on the latest about Kim. Are you going into college? Do you fancy meeting up for a coffee?"

Whoa, there! "I'm a bit caught up at the moment. Can't you tell me over the phone?" *That's tight*, she told herself.

After what he's done for us, you could at least meet him for coffee.

"She got the train to the airport," Lee told her. "She planned to take the next flight to Dublin."

"She really went?" Frankie checked. "So I can tell Marina she's out of the picture?"

"For sure," Lee confirmed. He seemed to want to get off the phone quickly now, and who could blame him? "See you, Frankie. Okay, bye."

Still feeling mean, she frowned and put down the phone, noticed a new message, and pressed "Play."

"One new message," the machine reported. "Message received Monday at 4:00 p.m."

Get a move on! Frankie's impatience with the slow, snooty machine voice almost made her switch off the message before it was delivered, but something made her hold on the extra second.

"Hi, this is a message for Frankie McLerran from Jessica West at the Bed-Head Agency. Frankie, another job for you, darling. I tried your mobile but there was no signal."

Damn! Frankie dug into her jeans pocket, dragged out her phone, and saw that the battery was flat.

"It's for tomorrow, Tuesday. No traveling involved—just local. Please give me a call."

Jeez! Automatically Frankie dialed the agency number. "Sorry, can't do it" were the words on her lips.

She got the receptionist, who put her straight through to Jessica.

"Frankie, where've you been? I've been tearing my hair out.

Listen, you've got one and a half hours flat to get yourself to the studio. It's local, at Number 35a Duchy Road. Don't worry, it's a short session—you should be in and out of there in three hours."

"Three hours!" Frankie cried. "I have to be in college. It's the show on Friday. My tutor will kill me!"

There was no hint of sympathy from the agency boss. Instead, she spun the usual line. "It's work, darling. There are a hundred girls lining up behind you, so grab it while you can."

Okay. So, first of all, Marina's in bits and she needs me. Second, I should, right this minute, be knocking on Claudia's door, taking in my pieces for the show. Third, I'm getting my ass kicked by Jessica. Once again, how the hell am I supposed to be in three places at once?

"Help!" Frankie said faintly. "Okay, I'll be there," she promised the agency boss.

"Thirty-five A Duchy Road, ten thirty," Jessica confirmed, before hanging up.

"Do your hair. Put on some lippy," Sinead advised. She considered telling Marina about Katrine's accident, but decided not to raise her hopes until Tristan had finally made up his mind. She'd never seen her like this before—totally drained and turned in on herself.

Slowly Marina shook her head. "I can't make it into college," she explained. "You go ahead. I'll stay here."

"By yourself?" Sinead shook her head. "No way."

"I'll be fine."

"No, you won't. If you stay in the house alone, you'll slide into a deep depression. I know. I've been there." She followed Marina from the kitchen into the front living room. "Try and make the effort," she advised.

But Marina couldn't battle the tears. She broke down again.

"Sit!" Sinead told her, plumping up the sofa cushions around her, then sitting cross-legged on the floor. "Talk to me. Tell me what's really bugging you."

"I don't know. I'm still shocked. This stuff happens to other people, not to me!" One minute Marina had a boring, middle-class family setup—two kids, two cars, two parents, plasma TV, and Smeg fridge-freezer—next minute everything was blown sky-high.

"Yeah," Sinead sighed. She knew that feeling from six years ago, when Daniella had split up with her dad. The kids were the victims, whichever way you cut it.

"And he lied!" Marina went on. "He wasn't even brave enough to tell the truth."

Sinead had been there too. "They think they're protecting you."

"Bollocks!" Marina dried her eyes.

Sinead nodded.

"He's an idiot."

"Yeah." Sinead uncrossed her legs and drew her knees up under her chin. "I expect he thinks he's in love. Being lost in the African bush, not knowing when you're going to get rescued—

it most likely brings a rush of blood to the head."

"Prat!" Marina muttered. She thought of worse words but didn't utter them.

"And your mum has probably been too complacent, taking him for granted, getting him to wash the car on a Sunday and mow the lawn."

"No, *she* does the garden," Marina argued, then shrugged. "Anyway, yeah, you're right. Mum's a bit of a control freak." *Lay the table, fill the dishwasher, ask permission before you sneeze.*

Sinead took her time, let Marina think her way through the situation, before she went on again in a low, soft voice. "This is not your mess," she convinced her. "Your life doesn't go on hold because of this."

Marina frowned, then took a deep breath. "You want me to go into college?"

Sinead nodded. "Today's Tuesday. The show is on Friday and you really should go and see Tristan. He might have some brilliant news for you."

"I'm not sure, Sinead. There's part of me that wants to curl up into a ball and make it all go away."

"And there's the rest of you that should be out there, still strutting your stuff," Sinead insisted. "Doing your Marilyn wiggle, making jaws drop, looking a million dollars."

Like they had when they first met—Frankie, Sinead, and Marina, dressing to kill and hitting the town, fabulous eye candy and proud of it, enjoying every second.

Marina nodded. She knew Sinead was right. "Where's Frankie?" she asked.

"Gone modeling. She says she'll meet us in college at one thirty."

"What time is it?"

"Eleven. That's two whole hours for you to shower and get ready to face the world, plus half an hour for us to walk into town."

"You'll wait for me?" Her face must look wrecked. She would need at least two hours to put it right.

Sinead nodded. She was secretly pleased with herself, thinking maybe she ought to train as a counselor, the way she'd brought Marina round. "Take a shower, do your hair, slap on the lippy!" she insisted. "Get your ass into college and show them what you can do!"

Fourteen

"The look is *Doctor Zhivago*!" Frankie's stylist for the day insisted. "It's romance and pre-Soviet Russia, it's starlight and snow!"

It's a wedding dress! Frankie thought. *Me in a Vera Wang white frock with a full-length white mink coat! I'm so-o-o hot!*

"Let's do this!" the photographer insisted, stepping back from the lights.

The stylist fiddled with Frankie's upswept hair. She tweaked the curls across her forehead then fixed a long flowing veil into the crown. "Moonlight!" she reminded Frankie. "Mountains and sleigh rides!"

Hot! Frankie struggled to stay cool inside the fitted fur coat. It was nipped in at the waist and gave only a glimpse of the bustier top and full satin skirt underneath. She stood in position and tilted her face toward the camera.

"Where's the groom?" the photographer snapped, looking beyond the screens toward a dark corner of the studio.

Groom? Frankie wondered. *No one mentioned a groom!*

A tall figure in a black frock-coat, gray silk shirt, and bootlace tie appeared from the shadows. His dark hair was shoulder-length. He wore cowboy boots and silver rings on every finger.

"Frankie, this is Mick," the stylist said.

The male model Frankie was marrying wore great aftershave. They leaned in toward each other and looked like they were in love. The photographer got to work.

"Lose the mink," the stylist instructed after a hundred or so shots.

Frankie loosened the coat and let it drop to the studio floor. It was twelve-thirty. She'd been here two hours already.

"Give me some body language!" the photographer ordered. "Come on, Frankie, look like you're getting married!"

Frankie gazed into Mick's amazing blue eyes. It was a crazy life, she thought, in her Vera Wang wedding dress. And how come these good-looking guys with square jaws and high cheekbones did nothing for her? She never felt any interest in the Mick look-alikes, not even a flicker.

"Whisper in his ear," the stylist told her. "Adore him. Make like this is the biggest, most romantic day of your life!"

Marina stared at her bare face in the mirror.

"Go ahead, you can do it!" Sinead urged. "Face first, then hair."

She started with foundation, smoothing it with her fingertips, brightening her dull cheeks with pink blusher. "Do I need concealer?" she asked anxiously.

"What's to conceal?" Sinead replied. "I don't see any shadows or wrinkles from where I stand."

Marina nodded and chose an emerald green eyeshadow.

"Not too much!" Sinead warned.

A touch of ivory shadow under the brow bone, and a smudge of kohl to outline the shape of her eyes. Marina leaned close to the mirror and applied the makeup with a steady hand.

"Cool!" Sinead told her. "Go for pale Bardot lips and big hair!"

"That'll take hours," Marina groaned.

But Sinead handed her the tongs and stood watch, hands on hips. Soon the volume was pumped up and Marina's blond hair fell in tousled waves. Then Sinead flung open Marina's wardrobe door. "Wear this," she suggested, pulling out a multicolored top from River Island—an off-the-shoulder style with pink, purple, and green zingy print on a white background, finishing in asymmetric layers, decorated with blingy sequins.

"What with?" Marina wanted to know.

Sinead dashed to her room and came back with a tie-dyed denim mini skirt. "Borrow this, with my pale blue espadrilles."

Marina put on the skirt but rejected the espadrilles. Seven pairs of shoes later, she settled on the espadrilles after all.

"Knockout," Sinead said, surveying the total package. She'd thrown on a long-sleeved, jade green chiffon top with a pair of frayed jeans, pulling spiky strands of hair over her forehead. The whole thing was spiced up with chunky coral beads. "You just worked a miracle!" she told Marina.

Marina inspected herself in the unforgiving mirror. She looked relaxed, sultry, and sexy. "I did!" she nodded.

"Ready?" Sinead checked.

Another nod. One final glance in the mirror. "Let's go!" Marina said.

Frankie left the studio at 1:15. Her bus was caught in traffic, so she didn't get to college until 2:00 p.m.

Sinead saw her dash in through the main entrance and went to meet her. "Where've you been?" she demanded.

Out of breath and still wearing the makeup from the photo shoot, Frankie explained that she'd been getting married.

"Frankie, you're not serious!"

"No—only kidding!" she quipped. "Hey, why the worried face? We're only five hours late for seeing Claudia!"

"Yeah," Sinead groaned. "And at least I got Marina into college while you were tying the knot. I left her in the cutting room, checking out leather samples for her shoe designs."

"Nice one," Frankie acknowledged. "I wouldn't have put money on it, the way she looked when I left the house this morning."

"We talked families. She got a lot out of her system." Walking down the corridor toward the jewelry tutor's room, Sinead felt a buildup of nerves. Not only were they half a day late, she wasn't sure she'd put enough work into writing down the theory and researching background for her body-art project. "Life's way too complicated," she complained. "Here's me, a year ago, thinking that coming to Central is my big chance to study fabulous fashion and give it one hundred percent."

"And what do we get?" Frankie agreed. "We get swamped by money problems, housing problems, men problems, Mum and Dad problems . . ."

"Which means we'll be lucky to get through this first year in one piece!" Sinead predicted, her hand trembling as she knocked at Claudia's door.

"No, we cannot have cable trailing across the middle of the room!" Tristan's voice had gone up a couple of octaves, showing dangerous stress levels to his unwilling volunteer helpers. "If it isn't long enough to go around the edges, we'll have to beg, borrow, and steal more extension leads!"

"I'll go back to my place and bring some," Rob offered. "And I've got plenty of gaffer tape. I'll fetch that too." He was back in college to set up his decks and be DJ for the opening.

Travis watched Rob shoot off on his errand, leaving him and Lee to take the flak from Tristan.

"This show must look totally professional—no trailing wires, no wonky, Mickey-Mouse partitions." Flapping here and there around the exhibition hall, Tristan placed numbered cards in each section to correspond with his new floor plan. "Travis, you're quite sure that your friend Rob knows what he's doing with all this electrical equipment?"

"Yeah, he's a professional DJ," Travis said calmly.

"In his dreams," Lee chipped in under his breath.

"As good as!" Travis mouthed. His job, now that the painters had finished, was to climb the ladders and set up the lights. In return, Tristan had promised Travis that he could show his reality TV project on a monitor in the entrance lobby where visitors came in.

"What's it called?" Tristan had asked doubtfully as Travis had given him a preview.

"'Pretty on the Outside.'" Travis had turned up the volume and waited for the Head of Department's reaction.

Tristan had watched only a couple of minutes before giving him the enthusiastic go-ahead. "Provided the girls in the film agree," he'd noted.

"They're cool," Travis had promised. And now he was doing Tristan the return favor of fixing the lights.

"How many people are on that list of invitations?" Tristan asked Lee.

Lee made a head count. "Ninety-three."

"And did all the invites go out on time? Do you think we need to swell the numbers, just in case the invited people don't show up?"

"Yes, they did, and yeah, I think it'd be good to put a few leaflets around college," Lee said, picking up on this because he was considering events management as a career option when he finished college. He wondered whether Tristan lost this much sleep over every First Year show. "Leave it with me. I'll knock up some extra publicity and make sure it gets distributed."

Travis frowned from the top of a ladder as yet another volunteer made his escape. Now he was the sole target of Tristan's neuroses.

"We need extra light in this area," came the next high-volume, high-pitched decision. "This is the spot where the showcase student will display her work. Talking of which . . ."

Tristan paused as the door swung open and Marina came in.

"Have you seen Sinead?" she asked Travis.

The sight of Marina made Travis wobble on top of his ladder. Marina wasn't exactly his type—too in your face, and anyway he didn't ogle other girls since he'd started going out with Sinead. But, wow, she looked stunning!

"Marina!" Tristan seized his chance. He swept toward her, carrying the holy of holies, the floor plan for Friday. "Just the person I needed to see!"

"I am?" she stammered. What was coming next?

"Yes, darling. Fortune is a fickle mistress!"

"It is?"

"She shines on a favored few."

Tristan seemed excited, but Marina couldn't understand a word of what he was going on about. In fact, all afternoon in college it had been a strain to keep a smile on her face and to concentrate on her leather samples and dyes. Now all she wanted to do was find Sinead and head on home.

"You are the chosen one!" Tristan explained.

Still Marina didn't get it.

"Think back to last week," he went on, dropping the fancy metaphor and coming down to her level. "You remember nagging me for more space?"

Marina nodded.

Tristan showed her his precious plan and pointed with his finger at the spot by the entrance. "You said you wanted this one."

Me and my big mouth! Now, after what was happening with her parents, the last thing she wanted was the stress of being given the prime location in the show.

"Well, you have it!" Tristan announced. "Katrine is still in the hospital, licking her mountaineering wounds. So it's over to you, Ms. Kent!"

"You're giving me the space?" she gasped.

From the top of his ladder, Travis gave her the thumbs-up.

"I am," Tristan confirmed. "Your designs will be showcasing the entire college," he warned. "So make the most of it, Marina. This is your big chance!"

"What happened to Wednesday?" Frankie asked.

It was just over twenty-four hours since Claudia had laid into them for being late yet again.

"No excuses!" she'd bawled. "I'm not interested. Sinead, you need to put in a lot more research. Frankie, your design sheets are garbage. Pretty photographs are not enough. In fact, the whole project is in danger of collapsing unless you both get your acts together!"

Neither Sinead nor Frankie had gotten much sleep. And all day today they'd been in the library and slaving over a drawing board, without even stopping for lunch.

Marina too had been choosing colors, printing out design sheets, and laminating display cards, readying for Friday.

"Any news from your folks?" Sinead asked, when she, Frankie, and Marina finally met up in the coffee bar at eight in the evening.

"Not a word," Marina replied. She didn't even want to think about what might be happening back at the old family homestead. Seeing Rob and the bike waiting for her in the street, she said a hasty good-bye to the girls.

"Are you meeting up with Travis?" Frankie asked Sinead. She felt almost too tired to put one foot in front of another to make her way back to Walgrave Square.

Sinead nodded. "Talk of the devil . . ."

Travis swung through the door and loped toward them with his loose, laid-back style. "Sorry, I'm late!"

"You're not." Sinead kissed his cheek then linked arms. "See you," she told Frankie.

Frankie sat and frowned into the dregs of her plastic cup. *Crazy life!* she sighed. *One minute I'm a bride in a designer dress, the next I'm playing Cinderella to Marina and Sinead!* No, poor comparison. Her two housemates were nothing like the Ugly Sisters. But it was true, right now she had nowhere to go.

When she looked up, Lee was standing by the counter with a pile of leaflets. He smiled at her.

"Can I have one of those?" Frankie asked.

"You can have as many as you like," he answered, delivering one to her table.

"Want a coffee?"

"Please."

Frankie went to fetch one while Lee sat down. Returning, she saw the back of his head and a hint of profile. Her stomach flipped.

What was that? she thought.

"Tristan's running around like a headless chicken," Lee told her, obviously filling a silence. "He thinks no one's going to come to the show."

For no particular reason, Frankie found herself staring at Lee's long eyelashes.

"Are your folks coming?" he asked, blushing.

"What? Oh, no. They live too far away. Too busy. Y'know."

"Hmm."

"How about yours? Oh, sorry, I forgot, you're a second year!" *Stoopid!* Her mind had gone to mush. What was going on here?

"Do you fancy helping me distribute a few trillion of these leaflets?" Lee asked, expecting a no.

Frankie sprang to her feet. "Yeah, cool!"

"Huh?" he frowned.

She grabbed a bundle and was set to sprint off and deliver. "Where am I taking them?"

"Local bookshops," Lee suggested. "And that little gallery opposite the bus stop. Places like that."

Frankie breathed in deeply then took the plunge. "Should we go together, or separately?"

He smiled as if he'd been waiting for this moment for a long time. "Together," he said quietly.

"He has gorgeous hands!" Frankie told Sinead and Marina when she got back to Number 13 late that night. "I always think you can tell a lot by a guy's hands. He's got these long, sensitive fingers and fantastic-shaped nails!"

"What's she drooling on about?" Marina asked.

Sinead yawned. "Who has gorgeous hands?"

"Lee, stupid! You should see his eyelashes. They curl up at the ends!"

"Lee who?" Sinead knew Frankie couldn't possibly mean Lee Wright from Travis's Moving Images course.

"Lee Wright! I went dropping off leaflets with him. I just got back. Haven't you been listening?"

"Lee *Wright*!" Marina and Sinead echoed. The Lee Wright whom Frankie had gone out with twice then spent the whole year dissing?

"He's cute," she insisted.

"Cute?" they said.

"Will you stop repeating every word I say?" Frankie glared at them. "And don't look at me like that. A girl can change her mind, can't she?"

"Yes," Marina and Sinead agreed. *At last, after all this time, all their wise words, and Frankie's pig-headedness—a result!*

"He's into old vinyl records. He's got a complete collection of Stones albums."

"You went to his place?" Marina gasped.

Frankie nodded. "After we'd finished dropping off leaflets about the show. We went there and had a beer."

"Did you snog him?" Sinead cut to the chase.

"Maybe," Frankie simpered.

"That means yes!" Marina cried. "Frankie snogged Lee—whoo-hoo!"

I did, Frankie thought, taking off her clothes and slipping under the duvet. *I did kiss Lee, and I don't know who was more gobsmacked—him or me.*

The sheets were cool on her skin. It was a nice thing to think about as she drifted off to sleep.

Lee handing her a Bud then turning on the seventies record player, hearing the needle hit the black shiny surface. Her snuggling up next to him on the floor cushions, him putting his arm round her shoulder.

Viewed from this miniscule distance, his face was out of focus, his eyes merging into one. His lips were soft. Maybe he kissed first, or maybe it was her.

"He's a fabulous kisser!" she could have told Marina and Sinead. They would have soaked up every detail.

But she'd kept it to herself and come to bed. Some things were just too good to share.

Fifteen

"All work and no play!" Sinead complained. She was running on empty, getting no sleep, still convinced she was going to fail.

"Tell me about it!" The floor of Frankie's room was invisible under sheets of design work. She loved making jewelry but she hated the theory part that Claudia had forced on her. "How long have we got?"

"Twenty-four hours. Tristan wants everything in place this time tomorrow." A day in the library loomed for Sinead. "Did we make a terrible mistake?" she asked Frankie. "I mean, is this the worst idea anyone ever had?"

"Hey, woman, don't go feeble on me now!" Frankie scrabbled on the floor to find a preliminary drawing of the arm band. "You'll soon be wishing you'd stuck to stretch-jersey mini dresses, satin skirts, and silk flowers!"

"Maybe," Sinead admitted.

"Boring!" Frankie scoffed. She seized the drawing and

spray-mounted it into her workbook. "We're cutting edge, baby. That's what we are!"

"Keep telling me that, in case I forget." Sinead sighed wearily.

"Cutting edge, cutting edge!"

"I'm out of here," Sinead said, closing the door on Crazy Girl.

`R u okay?` Marina read a text from her mother.

`Am fine,` she texted back. `How about u?`

`Okay here. Nothing decided yet xxxx`

Four kisses! Marina flipped her phone shut and sighed.

"They're manic!" Travis told Rob and Lee. "I just saw all three of them outside the library. Frankie's wearing her crazed look—wild eyes and hyper. Sinead's spouting stuff about woad and Native American war paint to anyone who'll listen."

"What about Marina?" Rob asked.

"Looks like she's not really there," Travis reported honestly. "In a kind of daze."

"Where are they now?" Lee wanted to know. He wasn't sure how to play it with Frankie since last night's kiss, pretty sure that with her it might be one step forward and two back like last time.

"Frankie's on her way to the jewelry lab. Sinead's burying her head in a book. Marina's been snaffled by Tristan."

The three guys stood aimlessly in the college entrance hall. Rob and Travis had finished their jobs of setting up the music, lights, and TVs; Lee had no more leaflets to give out.

"Beer?" Rob suggested.

"Might as well," Lee agreed.

"Game of snooker, anyone?" Travis led the way down the street to Escape. While the girls were feeling the pressure, the guys knew to stay clear.

"Cheyenne tribesmen, faces painted with white clay for sun dance." Sinead made a note under a photocopied print then put it in her folder. She had collected way too much information about the history of face and body painting throughout the world, but if Claudia wanted to see the background to her project, then background was what she would get. All that was left was to put it in some sort of order and present it on beautiful sheets of handmade paper, inside a folder decorated with the motifs Sinead had used in her own body art.

Eighteen hours to go! No time to eat. No time to find Frankie or Marina and see how they're getting on. Nightmare pressure! How much more can a girl take?

"Lapis lazuli, originally found in the foothills of the Himalayas," Frankie wrote under a sample of the raw, unpolished stone. "Very rare. Used in powder form to create blue dye in medieval illustrated manuscripts."

She wore her goggles pushed up onto her forehead, selecting other pieces of stone in various polished conditions. The color was amazing. She loved the perfectly smooth surface of the finished article, as well as the uneven roughness of the original object.

No time to stop and admire! she told herself. *I'm on the dreaded treadmill of assessment. I must not—repeat, must not—let Sinead down!*

"These are some of the most exquisite design sheets I have seen in a long time," Tristan told Marina. "The use of colored snakeskin is so contemporary, yet the retro feel is spot on too."

"Thanks." Quietly Marina collected the sheets spread out across the tutor's glass desk. She and Tristan had decided which ones to display and which samples to use. Tomorrow morning he would help her set them up in the exhibition hall.

"Relax," he told her. "Be happy."

"I am," she assured him. Once more, this was Tristan as she rarely saw him—considerate, complimentary, kind.

"You did a great job. You've been working under extra pressure this past week or two. I appreciate that."

Marina nodded. *Don't make me blub!*

"I take it your father got home safe and sound?"

"He's back in England," she confirmed, trying hard to swallow the tears.

"So maybe we'll see him at the show tomorrow?"

She shook her head. "I doubt it."

"No, okay. I expect he's still recovering from his ordeal."

"Something like that," Marina murmured. *Back off! Can't you see I'm on the edge? Look at me—I'm so not happy talking about this!*

*

"Marina, you didn't!" Frankie gasped.

"I did. I blubbed all over him." Marina was walking down the street with Frankie and Sinead, set to join Lee, Travis, and Rob in Escape. She wasn't proud of what had just happened—it had come over her without warning.

"What did Tristan do?" Sinead asked.

"Actually, he made with the box of tissues and said all the right stuff."

"You did the girly-tears thing with your Head of Department!" A cynical Frankie suspected Marina had been playing for sympathy.

"Not deliberately!" Marina protested. "They just welled up out of nowhere."

"Your tear ducts let you down." Sinead squeezed Marina's hand. "I know. I've been there."

"Saps!" Frankie scoffed, leading the way into the bar.

"I'll take you home," Rob told Marina the moment he saw her. Her eyes were red, she looked knackered.

"I'm okay," she insisted.

"She's so not okay!" Sinead argued.

"Let's go," Rob said. He walked her out of the bar, up the hill out of town.

"Why the tears?" he asked, his arm around her waist.

"Nothing. Everything." *My lousy family. My whole life.*

"Stay at mine?" he wanted to know.

Marina nodded. "I'll have to go back to my place in the morning to get ready though."

"Cool," he agreed, turning the key in the lock. "By the way, I got that job," he told her.

She broke out of her emotional doldrums and flung her arms around his neck. "Rob, you're kidding!"

"Nope. Tim Yorke rang me today and confirmed it."

"Oh babe! Oh Rob! That's amazing!"

He stepped out of her embrace, trying to be laid-back. "It's not that big a deal," he muttered.

"Rob, you're a real radio DJ! It's incredible. And I never even thought to ask!" She'd been so caught up in her own problems this past week. "When do you start?"

"Monday."

"That's soon. Oh God, I can't believe it! Wait till I tell the others!"

"I'm glad I can still make you smile," he told her with a grin, getting up close again. "Let's celebrate."

Marina kissed him. "How?" she whispered.

He didn't answer but led her upstairs. They went into his room and closed the door.

Rob was never one for talking—Marina knew this from the start. It was how he acted that mattered. And the way he looked at her when he kissed her, as if he never wanted to let her go.

"My place or yours?" Sinead asked Travis.

"You choose." After they'd left Frankie and Lee in Escape,

Sinead had insisted on taking a taxi to Walgrave Square.

"Mine," she decided, giving the driver the address and slumping back in the seat. "How totally wrecked am I!"

"Did you get through what you needed to do?" Travis trod on eggshells around the subject of tomorrow's show, in case Sinead threw a wobbler.

"I finished the research. Now all Frankie and I have to do is set up in the hall."

"Cool." Travis paid the taxi driver and held the car door for Sinead. "You're sure you want me to come in?" he checked.

"I'm so knackered I don't know what I want!"

"I could go back to my place." What he really wanted to do was lift her up and carry her into the house, wrap her in cotton wool, and look after her.

Sinead fixed him with a helpless look. "Travis . . . ," she murmured.

"Yeah, that's me."

". . . Thanks."

"For what?"

She was smiling, holding his hand, leading him into the house. "For everything. For you and me. For us."

"Show me my bed!" Frankie yawned. She and Lee were among the last customers to leave Escape. "Let me lay my weary head on my pillow!"

Lee held her upright as she swayed from side to side. "Are you okay?"

"Yeah, just kidding," she grinned. "But man, I'm tired!"

They began to walk hand in hand up Nugent Road, toward Lee's place. "Hey, and here's me thinking you were offering an invitation to join you!" he joked.

"Cheeky!"

"Pissed," he confessed.

"Really?"

"Nope. Stone-cold sober." Actually, somewhere in between.

"Hey, this is where you live!" Pointing out his doorway, Frankie looked ready to walk on alone.

"I'll take you home."

"You don't have to."

"I know I don't have to. I want to."

"Wow!" She cracked a smile from ear to ear. "That's so cool!"

Laughing, they walked on together. "Are you ready for tomorrow?" Lee asked.

"No way!" There were pictures to mount, text to print out, a zillion things still to do.

"Nervous?"

"Scared shitless," she admitted, her hand comfortably in his, matching stride for stride.

"Formal or casual?" Marina asked.

"Trousers or skirt?" Frankie appeared on the landing, wrapped in a bath towel.

"Prada or Chloe?" Sinead dithered.

". . . Formal," Marina decided. She would go for her Alexander McQueen, Edwardian look, in her ivory silk jacket with lace insert and matching silk skirt. Her hair would be loosely up and heavily backcombed. She came out of her room again to knock on Sinead's door. "Can I borrow your cream T-bar shoes?"

". . . Skirt!" Frankie made up her mind. She had a black mini exotically decorated around the hem with real pheasant and peacock feathers, which she teamed with an aubergine silk shirt and yellow and black crochet bead necklace down to her waist. "There's something missing!" she told her reflection. "I know—leather bracelets!"

". . . Missoni!" Sinead decided after all, picking out a turquoise, gold, and white creation made up of zigzag stripes, falling in soft folds below her knees. It was the real thing, courtesy of her mother.

"This is it!" Frankie declared at last. Her peacock feathers ruffled as she walked downstairs. "I'm ready. Let's go!"

"What do you think?" Marina posed, hand on hip, for Sinead.

"Decadent!" Sinead gave an approving nod. "Cool!"

"Get a move on up there!" Frankie yelled. One more minute and she would change her mind about going into college at all.

"I hate this dress!" Sinead decided.

"You look fine," Marina said.

Too late—Sinead had retreated into her room. She re-emerged two minutes later in a cropped red linen blazer with low-slung white cropped trousers and skinny snakeskin belt, carrying a gray felt trilby that she jammed on over her short blond hair.

"Let's go!" Frankie pleaded. "Please, I can't bear hanging around a second longer!"

So they gathered in the hallway and checked one another over. Marina smoothed in Sinead's blusher. Sinead told Frankie to get rid of two of her bangles. Marina and Frankie said Sinead was perfect, as usual.

"Ready!" Sinead declared.

This was it—the day of the show. They were looking their Burberry best, putting their Miu Mius where their mouths were.

"Ready!" Marina and Frankie agreed.

The door opened and the girls stepped out.

Sixteen

There was every color under the sun in the show, from rose to fuchsia, lemon to gold, peppermint to periwinkle. There was every conceivable style. Some students had gone hippie-trippy with a wild explosion of psychedelic patterns. Some had chosen romantic gypsy, with theatrical, outsize straw hats. There were featherlight fabrics hanging in long, loose layers; there were pleats and pin-tucks, jewels, sequins, and embroidery.

"Say hello to the new exotica!" Tristan declared, standing back from Daisy Fenwick's finished display of bold ethnic beads. "Come along, everyone—enter the souk in Marrakech!"

"How does it look?" an anxious Daisy asked fellow jewelry specialist Frankie.

"Wild!" Frankie told her. She and Sinead were putting the finishing touches to their own space, making sure their photographs were hanging dead level on the wall, dusting the plinth where Frankie's jewelry was displayed. In the center of their work, Sinead had arranged six white bowls of pure, powdered pigment—

cerise, cerulean blue, yellow ochre, crimson, violet, and magenta. The colors sang out and complemented the patterns painted on her body in the photographs.

"Nice touch," Claudia commented as she rushed by, carrying a stack of Katrine Walker knitwear, which she planned to display in her absence.

"More light!" From Marina's showcase space Tristan called for technical help.

Travis went running with extra spotlights, while Marina stood nervously to one side.

"Don't worry, babe, the Big Ego has landed!" Rob's comment on Tristan was geared to make Marina smile. "It all looks cool to me."

"Wine glasses!" Tristan announced suddenly. "Oh my God, did anyone order the wine glasses?"

"I did." Claudia deftly avoided disaster. "Plus sparkling water and fruit juice for the teetotalers."

"You're an angel," Tristan told her, weaving in and out of the displays, tweaking and ratcheting up an already tense atmosphere.

With the guests about to arrive, Rob checked the sound system. Travis altered the angle of the TV monitor above the entrance to the hall.

"Okay, that's it!" Sinead told Frankie after they'd made the final adjustments to their display. "No more arsing around. It's either good enough, or it isn't!"

Together they took a few steps back to study the effect.

"Oh God, I don't know!" Frankie was seized by panic. She wanted to run away and never stop.

"Me either!" Sinead groaned. The bottom line was—were they bravely experimental, or completely off their heads?

"Frankie, tell Tristan that we practically papered the city with leaflets!" Lee begged. "He won't listen to me!"

Instead she grabbed him and made him assess their work. "Lee, how does it look? Be honest!"

"Wow!" he said, genuinely amazed by the large, artful, beautifully mounted photographs, by the bowls of pigment, and by Frankie's blue and silver works of art.

"You mean it?"

He nodded. Then, as Rob played the first track, Lee pointed to the first visitors hovering by the doorway. "Here we go!" he warned.

Sinead and Frankie stood with their backs to the wall. They watched Tristan greet the visitors, saw Claudia offer them wine. Gradually the room filled up.

". . . Interesting!"

". . . Very contemporary!"

". . . So talented!"

Murmured comments passed between the guests.

"Who designed the gorgeous shoes?" one asked, demanding the Head of Department's attention.

Tristan drew Marina into the conversation while Sinead and Frankie watched from a distance.

"Hey!" Frankie cried. "That woman talking to Tristan right now—isn't that . . . ? Yes, it is—it's Daniella!"

"Darling, these are to die for!" Sinead's mother enthused, air-kissing her daughter's housemate. She had arrived in a cloud of Coco Mademoiselle, swathed in pale pink Sophia Kokosalaki like a Greek goddess. "I had no idea you were so talented."

A startled Sinead rushed across the crowded room. "Daniella, what are you doing here? Why didn't you tell me you were coming?"

Mwah! "It was a last-minute thing. I was in town unexpect-edly, so I thought I would come and support the show!"

"Go ahead, Sinead. Show Daniella your extraordinary work," Tristan told her.

"'Extraordinary' in a good or a bad way?" Daniella wondered out loud as Sinead reluctantly guided her through the brilliantly colored displays of fabrics and accessories.

Frankie gritted her teeth at their approach. She desperately wanted the ground to swallow her.

"Oh!" Daniella studied the photographs of her naked daughter, followed the lines of the swirling patterns painted on her skin, moved in to examine Frankie's stunning jewelry. For once in her life she had nothing to say.

"It's body art," Sinead explained nervously. "We believe the fashion world has gone as far as it can with stitching and drapery and so on. The future is in the past—it's in how we decorate the skin itself."

"Oh!" Daniella said again.

What was the verdict? Would she say that Sinead had wasted her own time and Daniella's money?

"She hates it!" Sinead mouthed at Frankie.

Frankie closed her eyes and held her breath.

"Absolutely beautiful!" Sinead's mother said at last. She wore a look of immense pride as she looked around the hall—*This is my daughter's work! See how unique and original it is!* "Utterly, utterly wonderful!"

Empty wine glasses stood on window ledges, the room was still buzzing, and Claudia was in animated conversation with a group of American visitors about Sinead and Frankie's work, when Marina beckoned them to her showcase space.

"What?" Frankie wanted to know. She was light-headed with praise and two large glasses of Cabernet Sauvignon.

"How's it going?" Sinead suspected that Marina too had been at the wine.

Marina didn't answer, but shoved them through the knot of people standing beneath the monitor that Travis had set up. Tristan was part of the small crowd, paying close attention to the content of Travis's film. "Watch this!" she hissed.

"I've already seen it," Sinead reminded her. The reality TV thing was old news with her.

"Not this bit!" Marina warned.

Frankie saw herself on-screen, shoulders back, hips swaying down the catwalk.

"*Pretty on the outside,*" Boz from Bad Mouth sang. "*Playin' to the crowd . . .*"

"What's wrong with that?" Sinead asked Marina.

"Watch!" Marina hissed.

There was a close-up of Frankie in the front room at Number 13, the sound of Sinead's voice saying, "Frankie's being a rebel," followed by Marina's, "She's being a pain in the ass."

Travis's camera zoomed in. "Get this, Travis!" Frankie said. "Why bother with silly qualifications and useless pieces of paper? All that matters is that you do the work that's important to you!"

In the audience gathered below the TV screen, Tristan smiled uneasily. The man beside him gave a small cough and shuffled his feet.

But Frankie hadn't finished yet. As Travis's camera went in for the kill, she stared into the lens. "On the record. I'm telling you that I'm boycotting the assessment!" she said.

"Whoa!" Marina on the screen gasped.

"What are you saying?" Sinead's voice demanded.

Frankie-on-screen tossed her dark hair while real-life Frankie felt faint. "I'm saying that Central Fashion College can stick their end-of-year show where the sun never shines!"

"Travis!" Frankie, Sinead, and Marina found him standing by the sound system with Rob and Lee. They surrounded him and pinned him against the window.

"You louse!" Marina said.

Sinead followed up with one word—"Judas!"

"I thought you were my friend!" Frankie cried.

"Why? What did I do?"

"You filmed me telling everyone they could stick their assessment up their ass!"

"Ah!" Travis didn't try to defend himself.

"Tristan just saw her!" Sinead told him.

"And so did everyone else in this room!" Marina added.

Lee and Rob stood with arms folded. They watched the ambush without moving a muscle.

"It's not looking good for Trav," was Lee's opinion. "My guess is, he's about to suffer for his art!"

"Unless . . ." Rob's glance had strayed across the room to where the Head of Department was greeting a couple of latecomers. Suddenly Travis's problem slipped from center stage.

"Unless what?" Marina left off harassing Travis. She turned to see Tristan shaking hands with her mum and dad, as if everything in the world was hunky-dory. "Oh my God!"

Sinead and Frankie watched her drift across the room in a daze.

"So good to see you!" Tristan was telling Martin Kent. "Marina will be thrilled you could make it!"

Alice made the first move toward their daughter. "Surprise!" she said with a wry smile.

"What happened? What are you doing here?"

"We dropped Tom off at school and then thought we would call in here."

"No, I mean, what happened!" Marina pointed to her dad and then her mum, to and fro several times.

"Still nothing definite," her mother told her in a low voice. "We're talking things through."

Martin Kent prised himself away from Tristan and came to join them. "You got the star spot!" he crowed. "Mr. Fox tells me you're a shoe designer who's definitely going places!"

"Weird!" Frankie said to Sinead, viewing the family reunion from across the room. "It looks like the Kents are back together."

Sinead studied the body language. Mrs. K was looking good in black—Escada-style double-breasted jacket, slim trousers, high patent shoes. Mr. was more casual in moccasins and polo shirt. His hands were in his pockets. Her back was turned toward him. "I wouldn't bet on it," she said quietly.

"Did he tell her about Kim?" Frankie wondered.

Sinead shook her head. "Would you?"

"Nope."

". . . Yeah well, definitely watch this space," Sinead agreed.

"Did you tell Mum about Kim what's-her-name?" Marina split her dad from her mum and got him in a corner.

"Not yet," he confessed.

"Are you going to tell her?"

"I don't know. Like I said, I don't want to hurt her."

Marina rolled her eyes. "Don't give me that again! Listen, are you staying with Mum, or leaving her?"

He shrugged. "We're talking it through."

"Don't give me that either!" She knew they couldn't speak for long and she had definite things to say. This time she wouldn't lose it with him but just speak her mind. "Dad, this isn't rocket science. If you're planning on staying, don't ever mention that woman's name again, under any circumstances, and I won't either!"

"You won't?" he frowned.

"I won't," Marina promised. "On the other hand, if you want to leave and break up the whole family and lose everything you've worked for all your life, just say the name Kim Cosgrove, then stand back and wait for the shit to hit the fan!"

"So cool!" Frankie was impressed.

"Babe, we're proud of you!" Sinead told her. "You're the twenty-first-century chick, telling it like it is!"

No one was left in the exhibition hall except for Frankie, Sinead, and Marina. The lights were dimmed, the shadowy displays shimmering and glittering under the orange street lamps.

Marina half sighed, half smiled. Sinead was right—it felt good to have laid it on the line for her dad. Now her boring, half-baked, shortsighted parents (but face it, the only parents she had) would have to sort out their own mess, however they chose.

"Will they stay together or split?" Frankie wondered.

"Who knows?" Marina walked between the draped mannequins, the tables spread with fabrics, the jewelry, and the shoes. "*Que sera sera!*"

"Whatever will be will be," Sinead interpreted. She knew the song well. Doris Day circa 1950s:

> "*When I was just a little girl,*
> *I asked my momma, what will I be.*
> *Will I be pretty, will I be rich?*
> *Here's what she said to me . . .*"

"*Que sera sera!*" Marina and Sinead sang together a sweet, lilting song from Marina's favorite decade.

> "*Whatever will be will be,*
> *The future's not ours to see . . .*"

"Cheese-tastic!" Frankie laughed. "I can tell you what *my* future is . . . !"

Sinead and Marina followed supermodel Frankie out of the room, down the empty corridor, out of the building.

"My future is—a Bacardi Breezer in Escape!" Where they would meet up with Travis, Rob, and Lee.

Sinead caught up with Frankie. "A summer in New York!" she predicted. "Your face on all the front covers."

"With Rob as a top DJ!" Marina dreamed. "And me making shoes for Charles Jourdan!"

"And Travis filming 24/7!" Sinead's view was less rosy. She saw a summer of hiding in the loo from the prying lens, until she looked up one of Daniella's contacts and swanned off on work experience.

"Me and Lee doing the traveling thing in Eastern Europe!" Frankie forecast. "Prague, Budapest, Bucharest . . ."

Marina and Sinead pounced on her. "You and Lee?" Marina cried.

"About time!" Sinead yelled what she and Marina had always thought. "Lee and Frankie get it together. It's fate! It's karma!"

"Whoa there, steady on!" Frankie pulled herself free. The bar was in sight. Travis was waiting inside with Lee and Rob for the girls to carry on giving him a hard time.

But before they went into Escape, they stopped on the pavement.

"We made it!" Frankie grinned. "We did a whole year in fashion college!"

"We did!" Marina agreed. "We had our down times . . ."

"And our ups," Frankie insisted.

"We came through," Sinead sighed. It was a moment to hang on to, on the broad pavement outside the bar, with the red brake lights of the cars winking and guys leaning out of the windows. *Hey, girls!*

"Whoo!" Frankie's grin was broad.

Marina waved at the good-looking guy in the Porsche.

They made their entrance into Escape. At the last moment, Sinead turned, took off her stylish felt hat, and flung it high into the night sky.